CHECK 4 cd's

W9-AUG-251

Posing as People

Three Stories, Three Plays

_____
Orson Scott Card

_____
Scott Brick

_____
Aaron Johnston

_____
Emily Janice Card

Posing as People

Three Stories, Three Plays

Posing as People

Three Stories,
Three Plays

Orson Scott Card

Scott Brick | Aaron Johnston | Emily Janice Card

SUBTERRANEAN PRESS | 2004

Hatrack River Publications

First Edition

ISBN
1-59606-015-8

Subterranean Press
PO Box 190106
Burton, MI 48519

www.subterraneanpress.com
www.hatrack.com

FOREWORD

by Orson Scott Card

When I was a theatre student in college, I discovered the power of playwriting. I could take existing stories, find the key scenes, put them on stage, turn actors loose with my dialogue, and audiences would laugh, cry, get excited—right where I wanted them to.

As I watched the audiences watch my plays, I could see exactly how the plays worked—and exactly where they didn't. Audiences don't lie while they're watching. If the play is working, they don't look away, they don't twitch, except to laugh or cry on cue. Only when the play *isn't* working do they notice that they need to cough or that they have an itch or that they're sore from sitting so long.

So when they shift in their seats or turn to whisper to a neighbor or cough, there's something wrong with the play.

Bad playwrights blame the actors or the director. Or the rainy night or the set or the costumes or the heat or the cold.

Good ones recognize that it's the playwright's duty to write an actor-proof script. Good playwrights know that ultimately, it's between the writer and the audience.

At the same time that I was learning these things as a playwright, I was also going to the university bookstore and hanging out in their tiny science fiction section. Since I was broke, there were few times I could buy anything; and I didn't have the chutzpah to sit there and read an entire book in the store. Now and then I'd buy a novel or story collection. Arthur C. Clarke. Isaac Asimov. Robert A. Heinlein. Andre Norton. Ray Bradbury. Zenna Henderson.

I visited there, day after day, to stare at the newly published hardcover of Ray Bradbury's *I Sing the Body Electric*. I couldn't afford it. But I knew I wanted it. I wanted to be inside the worlds of the man who wrote *Dandelion Wine* and *The Martian Chronicles* and *October Country* and *Something Wicked This Way Comes*.

And I wanted something else. I wanted to be able to do for other readers what they had done for me.

By no means was science fiction my sole reading. Herman Hesse, Ayn Rand, James Michener, J.R.R. Tolkien, John Hersey—all the writers that college undergraduates were reading in those days, I read.

But the science fiction writers were the ones who created whole worlds out of nothing. I wanted to do what they did.

So I invented a world where a hereditary strain of mental powers was being nurtured on an obscure farm deep in the Forest of Waters. A handful of stories: "The Tinker," "Worthing Farm," "Worthing Inn."

I had no idea what I was doing with this fiction, though; I couldn't really audience-test it. I couldn't sit there and watch people read, see how they responded, find out what was working and what wasn't.

So, when I was 19, I tried my hand at a science fiction play. "The Fairy Godfather" was my attempt, written in longhand in a spiral-bound notebook, as all my plays were in those days. I thought it was very innovative—but only because I hadn't read all that much science fiction at the time.

I knew the limitations of the stage. I didn't want to write plays that required there to be elaborate attempts to visualize future settings. This was before *Star Wars*, so I was quite familiar with how wretched sci-fi settings always looked, even on the big screen. The monsters of *Outer Limits* always looked pretty silly, and *Star Trek* was melodramatic and badly acted and looked cheap. I didn't want to create science fiction that looked like that.

I had earlier tried another science fiction play—this time very dark and allegorical and post-apocalyptic, called *No Fall Next Time* and then *The Pit*. It was very philosophical and edgy—just what undergraduates were supposed to be writing during the Vietnam War. That was what I showed the agent from MCA who came to my school to interview students. He was full of all the changes that needed to be made so that *The Pit* would work as a movie. I told him I wasn't interested in making it a movie, I wanted it to be a play. He told me I was insane. I couldn't disagree.

I also couldn't finish *The Pit*. But I did finish *The Fairy Godfather*.

Then I went on my two-year mission to Brazil. While I was there, I kept working on my Worthing stories, developing the concepts that would eventually lead to *Capitol* and *Hot Sleep*, which later became *The Worthing Saga*. But when I turned my hand to playwriting while on my mission, it was scripture from which I drew my stories—that's when I wrote *Stone Tables*, the most successful play of my college writing career, despite its flaws.

While I was on my mission, though, my younger brother asked if he could direct *Fairy Godfather* at Orem High School, with Bruce Cunningham playing the lead and an extraordinarily talented Canadian actress named Janet Scott doing the recorded voice of the computer. It happened that it was put on right after I got home from Brazil, and so we turned it into a workshop, inviting audience members to stay and comment.

The responses were generally positive, but I already knew the truth: I had been watching the audience. The play didn't really work. It was too talky, too inactive. Too much had to be explained.

I decided then and there that science fiction plays didn't work. Or if they did, they had to be a very special *kind* of play, and I'd be better off writing my science fiction as stories and using plays for different purposes. From then on I concentrated on musical theatre on the one hand, and narrative science fiction on the other. And never the twain should meet.

Skip thirty years.

My daughter Emily, by then in her early twenties, was reading some of my short stories. (We've never required our kids to read any of my fiction, and if they do, we never try to discuss it with them. They last thing they need is to believe that liking my work is a test of family loyalty.) I assumed that she was reading them for the first time—only when I read the afterword she wrote for the publication of her play in this book did I learn that she had read the story much earlier.

So I suppose she was *re*reading "Sepulchre of Songs," and she came downstairs and told me this great idea she had for how "Sepulchre" could be staged.

It *was* a great idea.

And for the first time it dawned on me that maybe the reason *Fairy Godfather* didn't work was because it wasn't a good story in the first place. That the problem wasn't that sci-fi didn't work on stage, it's that *that story* didn't work *anywhere.*

After all, I had never been tempted to turn it into narrative fiction, even after I reached a point in my career where almost anything I wrote could get published. I didn't believe in that story, or I would have used it.

Emily's idea was proof that no obstacle was insurmountable. And since my stories are still almost always plays-in-disguise—consisting mostly of dialogue and veiled stage directions—maybe they *could* work on stage.

If they were written by somebody besides me. Because I not only didn't have time, I also didn't trust myself to be able to get past that bias that I'd developed after *Fairy Godfather.* So I told her: You write that script, and I'll find a couple of other writers and we'll do a program of one-act plays based on stories of mine.

She agreed, and we were off.

I turned to Aaron Johnston and Scott Brick almost at once. I first met Scott Brick when, as a freelance writer, he interviewed me for a magazine article. We hit it off so well on the telephone that we got together for ice cream (the Mormon equivalent of "having coffee") and from then on were friends. Even after he got the gig to write the screenplay for *Rendezvous with Rama* and my envy of him nearly killed me, we were friends.

Scott was a natural for this because he loved and understood science fiction, he knew my work, and he knew theatre, being an actor with loads of experience in the LA scene, including his extraordinarily good work as a voice actor on audiobooks. (Though he urges me to tell you that the *Wall Street*

Journal article about him in November of 2004 wildly inflated his earnings from voice acting. It does *not* pay that well.)

I had also directed Scott as Gandalf in my authorized reader's theatre production of *The Lord of the Rings* at a Mythopoeic Society conference at Pepperdine—I knew something of what he could do on stage and how he responded to my style of direction.

When I invited him to take part, Scott chose the story "Clap Hands and Sing," and proceeded to transform it in ways I would never have imagined. For one thing, he faced the same problem that I had faced with *Fairy Godfather*—most of the dialogue was between a very old man who hardly moved…and a computer. Dull! Boring! Nothing to see!

Unlike me, however, Scott thought of what now seems the obvious solution. Not a computer, an android: a character that can be played by an actor. And then when he had the further insight of having the android become the young version of the old man during the time travel sequence, I was blown away. He used highly theatrical techniques to illuminate the story in ways that narrative fiction could not.

Aaron Johnston spent some of his teenage years near where my family lives in Greensboro. I saw him perform the part of the Big Bad Wolf in a church production when he was in his teens; and then, after college, he and his bride, Lauren, came back to North Carolina and did a part in a talent show I was emceeing. They were brilliant comedians; the audience was screaming and crying with laughter. After the show I found out they had been part of a professional improve comedy troupe in Provo, Utah, and I realized that what I was seeing with the two of them was not just talent, but genius.

I began to work with them at every opportunity. They played Algernon and Cecily in my production of *The Importance of Being Ernest*; I used them to play Jimmy and Snookie in *110 in the Shade*. And when they moved to Los Angeles, I began to work with Aaron on filmscript adaptations of some of my novels. We also are collaborating on a novel version of my short story "Malpractice," based on his screenplay.

No surprise, then, that I asked him to pick a story and try adapting it for stage.

Emily, too, I had known as a writer all her life—it's not just a proud father who knows her as an extraordinarily gifted poet, essayist, and fiction writer. I also worked with her as an actress. When I saw that neither the local high schools nor the community theatres were blessed with directors who had the faintest idea how to teach technique to young actors, I started teaching her myself, directing her in such parts as Luisa in *The Fantasticks*, Lizzy Curry in *100 in the Shade*, the Ann-Margret part in *Bye-Bye Birdie*, Gwendolyn in *The Importance of Being Ernest*, and Princess Winnifred—the Carol Burnett part—in *Once Upon a Mattress*.

By the time she took on adapting "Sepulchre of Songs," I knew she was not only ready to write the play, she was also ready to play the extraordinarily difficult role of the armless, legless girl in the hospital bed.

The idea was that all three of the writers would also play a major role in their own plays. It almost worked that way. Scott played Jock/Young Charlie in "Clap Hands," and Emily played Elaine/Anansa in "Sepulchre." But before casting was set, Aaron and Lauren found out they were going to be the parents of child number two—and that his probable day of birth was during the run of the show. Aaron did not want to be in the position of choosing between "The show must go on" and "The father of all my future children will be present at the birth of this one," so the part of Hamilton was not his after all.

Instead, he produced the whole show and slept only three hours, I believe, in the last week before the opening.

I read the scripts when they turned them in, made suggestions where appropriate, but what I did *not* do was go back and read the short stories they were adapting. Since I was directing these plays, I wanted to treat them as I always wanted to be treated as a playwright. I was not going to try to second-guess their adaptations and try to be "true" to my original. I was going to direct *their scripts* and let my stories take care of themselves. After all, a good adaptation doesn't erase the original. Anybody who wanted to see my version could read it. When they came to *Posing As People*, they were going to see a production of these writers' scripts.

So my suggestions were as director of their plays, not as the author of the original stories. I didn't have that many suggestions anyway—the scripts were terrific. They absolutely worked.

Our casting went well, also. We already had enough of a network of friends that we didn't bother with open auditions, though everyone did try out before getting their parts. Friends of friends—but nobody was brought into the cast who wasn't, in a word, wonderful. Los Angeles is an amazing trove of acting talent; you have to be brain dead as a director—or have a lousy script—not to be able to find brilliant actors and help them do great performances. I'm not brain dead, we had excellent scripts, and so these actors gave extraordinarily good performances.

The scripts as published in this volume are almost exactly as they were performed, so you're getting the benefit of the revisions that occurred during rehearsals and performances. But those revisions were all either originated or approved by the authors of the revisions. In movies, the director may be king, but in theatre in America, the playwright gets the last word.

The nice thing is that you don't have to take my word for how good these performances were. Before the run of the show ended, Stefan Rudnicki, who played Charlie in "Clap Hands," took the cast to a recording studio and laid down a complete cast recording of all three shows. The result is the CDs that accompany this book, which include not only the plays as performed by the original cast, but also readings of the short stories.

Which is why I don't need to praise the cast members one by one: They will speak for themselves far more eloquently through their performances.

ORIGINAL CAST

Posing As People opened in Los Angeles on 10 September 2004 at the Whitefire Theater with the following cast:

CLAP HANDS AND SING

Lawyer 1 ....Eric Artell
Lawyer 2 ....Sara Ellis
Sportscaster ....Lara Schwartzberg
Lucy Host ....Sara Ellis
Ronco Pitchperson ....Victoria Von Roth
News Anchor..........................Kelly Lohman
Charlie ....Stefan Rudnicki
Jock...Scott Brick
Rachel Carpenter ....Emily Janice Card
Mrs. Carpenter......................Victoria Von Roth

LIFELOOP

Arran Handully......................Lara Schwartzberg
Felice.......................................Kelly Lohman
Hamilton ....Eric Artell
Truiff.......................................Victoria Von Roth
Technician ....Scott Brick

A SEPULCHRE OF SONGS

Therapist ....Kirby Heyborne
April..Kelly Lohman
Elaine......................................Emily Janice Card
Doug..Eric Artell
Wallace....................................Stefan Rudnicki
Becky ....Lara Schwartzberg

Directed by Orson Scott Card
Produced by Aaron Johnston
Lighting by Derrick McDaniel
Designed by Cristian Bell

Three Plays

CLAP HANDS AND SING

a one-act play by
Scott Brick
based upon the short story by
Orson Scott Card

INTRODUCTION

by Scott Brick

When Scott Card asked me to adapt one of his short stories for the stage, I, of course, was flattered, and played coy for all of about a nanosecond. "Well, do I get to choose the story?" I asked, assuming a hauteur I couldn't quite pull off. When Scott said "Yes, absolutely," I blurted out "Clap Hands and Sing" before he could finish speaking.

The idea for this evening of one-acts, of course, began when Emily Card told her father that she'd come up with a lovely stage device that would seamlessly adapt one of his stories that had previously been thought of as unadaptable. My own choice of story had little to do with how well it might translate to the stage, however, and had nothing to do with the stage convention I would ultimately employ to adapt it. Rather, it had only to do with being true to what I felt when I first read the story, many years before.

Simply put, when I first read "Clap Hands and Sing," I cried. Rather, I *wept*. So struck was I by its inherent loveliness and the message of indelible love it conveyed (and Scott's poetic way of conveying it) that I immediately thought, "I would love to share this story with as many people as possible, I would love for them to feel what I'm feeling now." *Posing As People* was the means to that end. Choosing to adapt this story was merely my attempt to remain true to my thoughts and feelings at the time, and offer this beautiful story to people who might not otherwise read it.

After our initial performance, an audience member approached me and told me how much she wept after seeing the show, and how much its message impacted her. I thanked her, smiled, and thought, "One down, the rest of humanity to go…!"

Dedication

*To Mike Frym,
teacher, mentor and friend –
I still say thanks, every night.*

Cast of Characters

CHARLIE—approximately 90 years old

JOCK—30s, a robotic, idealized version of Charlie

YOUNG CHARLIE—early 20s

RACHEL CARPENTER—eight years younger than Young Charlie

MRS. CARPENTER—dowdy and delightful, Rachel's mother

LAWYER 1—sycophant, yet daring

LAWYER 2—sycophant, yet… well, nothing else, just a petrified sycophant

VIDEO SCREEN PERSONALITIES: SPORTSCASTER, LUCY HOST, RONCO PITCHMAN, NEWS ANCHOR, FDA ANNOUNCER, CLINICIAN

Video images are seen throughout the play. As written, these images are to be performed live, suggesting a 3D holographic broadcast unit, yet when budgets allow, they can be presented on actual screens.

The date of October 28, 2004, as well as days of the week referenced in the script, should be updated to reflect current production dates. The past referred to in the play should always be our present.

Quotations from William Butler Yeats: "Sailing To Byzantium" (1927), "Among School Children" (1927).

Scene One

At Curtain's Rise, the stage is dominated by Charlie's room. A typical setup for an aging, hospitalized invalid—typical, that is, of multi-billionaires. Furnishings are lavish, with various elaborate diagnostic/therapeutic machines sitting near the bed. Clearly this is no sterile hospital; it is the luxurious private residence of an extremely wealthy man.

Stage setup should suggest a large video screen sitting in front of Charlie's bed, although the audience sees its images behind him: Charlie faces outward, as though watching the screen; FLICKERING LIGHTS behind him suggest the pictures, a stage representation of the holographic images he beholds. The flickering lights bathe Charlie's bed in their soft glow.

LIGHTS UP SLOWLY to reveal CHARLIE in a wheelchair next to his bed. Dressed in baggy pajamas, he sleeps, completely unaware of the images before/behind him. A remote control is barely visible beneath his thigh.

TWO LAWYERS stand facing the screen, part of a video conference in progress. They fidget, twiddle pens in their grasp, nervously shift papers, etc., not yet realizing the old man has fallen asleep.

> LAWYER 1
> …only so long we can hold them off, sir. The President insists he can't keep the Oversight Committee from investigating the THIEF program.

> LAWYER 2
> We've put pressure on him to keep his boys in line…

> LAWYER 1
> …but it's bi-partisan, I'm afraid. His hands are tied.

> LAWYER 2
> And the media are insisting you either step down as CEO or name a successor.

> LAWYER 1
> MurdochNewsNet has been suggesting that actor, what's his name? The really old one…

> LAWYER 2
> But we can handle that, that's the least of our worries. The real problem…um…

They look at one another in fear. No one wants to drop this bomb.

> LAWYER 1
> Sir, the Minority Leader just called for deregulation.

There's a pause.

> LAWYER 2
> We don't have the votes to stop it.

Both lawyers await a blow-up that never comes.

> LAWYER 1
> It would affect all of THIEF. The entire program, sir.

The lawyers exchange anxious glances, then face the screen again, expectantly.

> LAWYER 2
> Not just the time-travel platform…

> LAWYER 1
> (mutters, disgusted)
> He's asleep again.

> LAWYER 2
> (louder)
> …but the, uh, ancillary programs, as well.

Lawyer 1 waves his hands before the "camera," and when there's no response, shrugs and rolls his eyes.

> LAWYER 1
> He can't hear you.

> LAWYER 2
> (louder still)
> Sir, it's time travel in the hands of the masses. The great unwashed, sir.

Lawyer 1 chuckles, nudges Lawyer 2, then points to the screen as if to say, Watch this.

> LAWYER 1
> Sir, the Board just approved a 100% increase in the Charitable Contributions program—the, uh, jaunts for the

poor but otherwise worthy? Yeah, so there will actually be *two* free trips through time next year, sir.

Lawyer 2 laughs unexpectedly, then stifles the sound when he hears it.

> LAWYER 2
> You can't say that…

> LAWYER 1
> Sir, Wall Street wags saw smoke rising from corporate head-quarters and have been making comparisons to the Vatican…

> LAWYER 2
> (to Lawyer 1)
> You're going to wake him up…!

> LAWYER 1
> …they say you're at death's door and we're desperately try-ing to elevate some poor Cardinal.

> LAWYER 2
> Actually that one's true, sir…

> LAWYER 1
> (to Lawyer 2)
> Y'know, we should just reprogram that android of his and stick him in the old guy's place, a kinda "Man in the Iron Mask" kinda thing.

> LAWYER 2
> (petrified)
> Shhhh! Don't wake *that* one up…!

Charlie rolls over slightly in his chair, activating the remote control. WHITE NOISE signifies the changing of a channel. LIGHTS DOWN on lawyers. LIGHTS UP on new image. (Each subsequent video image will be in separate stage areas, sequentially lighted as the channels change.)

> SPORTSCASTER
> …in Mega Bowl IX! Your final once again: Pittsburgh Steelers 62, Manchester United 6. No field goals or missed extra points, by the way—the Brits managed three safeties when Pittsburgh couldn't handle the newly-sanctioned ball in the end zone—

More WHITE NOISE, and again the channel shifts. The "I Love Lucy" theme is heard.

> HOST
> …as we celebrate the show's 120th anniversary by counting down your favorite 120 episodes, here on The Lucy Channel…!

Another channel shift.

> RONCO PITCHMAN
> …Ronco's new ACTIVE MOM, the convenient electric breast pump that stores up natural mother's milk so your baby will feel your love all the time. ACTIVE MOM, because no matter how busy you are, your baby comes first…

Another channel shift:

> NEWS ANCHOR
> …today called for drastic censorship of Lifeloops, urging Hollywood to stop what the Moral Minority have termed an "ugly" and "profane" practice, and remove all cameras from toilet bowls, urinals and bidets…

Another channel shift: a man and woman lewdly embrace, while an ANNOUNCER delivers an FDA warning.

> ANNOUNCER
> JACKHAMMER should not be used by anyone taking aspirin, sleep aids or cold suppressants. Do not take JACKHAMMER in conjunction with anabolic steroids. If you're in a monogamous relationship, avoid taking JACKHAMMER while trying to get pregnant. JACK-HAMMER should not be used by epileptics, diabetics, narcoleptics, heart patients, people with allergies, hay fever or stomach disorders. May cause shingles, gas and intensive vomiting…

Charlie opens his eyes and the commercials cease abruptly, replaced by an image of RACHEL. Charlie's eyes open blearily, yet before they can focus on Rachel, her image disappears, replaced by another rabid pitchman—this time, however, the image is silent, MUTED. Instead, the TV emits an obnoxious announcer's voice:

> TV VOICE
> It's late.

>   CHARLIE
>   (growls)

>   TV VOICE
> It's late.

>   CHARLIE
> Shut up.

>   TV VOICE
> It's late.

>   CHARLIE
> Shut up!

>   TV VOICE
> It's late.

Charlie grips the remote to hurl it at the TV.

>   JOCK
> You fell asleep in front of the television again, Charlie.

JOCK moves, and we realize it's his voice we've been hearing. He has been sitting silently, motionless, since the curtain's rise, yet his posture has been that of an android in powersave mode, his head down, hopefully unnoticed by the audience. Jock is the most elaborate and effective of Charlie's diagnostic/therapeutic machines. His demeanor and attitude should suggest a younger, more idealized version of Charlie. Jock powers up now and stands. His appearance is entirely human, yet the occasional stiff movement should convey he's an android.

>   CHARLIE
> Leave me alone, swine.

>   JOCK
> Don't fall asleep in front of the television, Charlie.

>   CHARLIE
> Okay, turn it off.

Charlie waves absently at the screen and it begins to fade. In the flicker, Charlie once again sees the image of RACHEL before lights completely fade. Charlie questions the images in his mind rather than the screen.

CHARLIE
Who…?

JOCK
What?

CHARLIE
That was…

JOCK
You've been tuned to:
(rapidly)
CNN, CNBC, Lucy, A&E, Spice, Bravo, History, BET—

CHARLIE
(shakes his head)
Who did that remind me of?

JOCK
I'm not programmed to read your mind, Charlie.

CHARLIE
Juliet? No. She *played* Juliet.

JOCK
It's time for your meds again.

CHARLIE
…Rachel.

JOCK
No, *you* have to take them this time.

CHARLIE
Rachel Carpenter.

Jock inserts his hand into a computer interface. He cocks his head as though rapidly downloading data.

JOCK
You've got mail! Your lawyers have forwarded seventeen documents for your signature, you have two injections waiting for your perforated arms, and a news upload awaiting your haggard face, so we can prove to one and all that you are, indeed, alive.

CHARLIE
I'm tired, Jock.

JOCK
Yet will they capture the irony in a man building a fortune
on time machines…

CHARLIE
Let them wait, I said I'm tired.

JOCK
…only to survive long enough to find out that every aged
person is his own time machine? I somehow doubt this. Here.

*Jock moves to help Charlie out of his wheelchair. On unstable legs, Charlie stands
while Jock places a bathrobe around his shoulders. Jock kneels. With his back to
the audience and leaning on Jock's shoulders, Charlie steps into a pair of paja-
ma bottoms.*

JOCK
"An aged man is a paltry thing, a tattered coat upon a stick."

CHARLIE
Shut up.

JOCK
"Unless Soul clap its hands."

CHARLIE
I said shut up!

JOCK
"And sing, and louder sing, for every tatter in its mortal dress."

CHARLIE
Are you finished?

JOCK
You know I am. You programmed me.

CHARLIE
Bad enough I made you *look* like me…

JOCK

I used to wonder what effect my facial features would have on any of your old friends who dropped by to visit. Until I discovered you don't have any friends.

Charlie doesn't respond. He climbs into bed, painfully, using a cane propped against the bed.

JOCK

What's wrong?

CHARLIE

Nothing.

JOCK

You're going to bed without complaint. What's wrong?

CHARLIE

Ah yes, dear computer, a change in the routine of the habit-bound old man, and you suspect what, a heart attack? Incipient death? Extreme disorientation? Don't hold your breath, I'm fine.

JOCK

What's wrong, Charlie?

CHARLIE

A name. Rachel Carpenter.

JOCK

Living or dead?

CHARLIE

I don't know.

Jock again places his hand inside the computer interface.

JOCK

Living and dead, I have one thousand four hundred eighty in the company archives alone.

CHARLIE

She was…seven years younger than me. Eight? And she lived in Provo, Utah. Her father was a pianist. Quite famous, actually. Everyone always angled for an invitation to their home…

LIGHTS UP on RACHEL, standing behind Charlie, speaking to him as if from across the years.

> RACHEL
> My father is always the main attraction. Our living room is like a cluttered salon, and there are always many admirers. But you came to see *me.*

LIGHTS DOWN on Rachel.

> CHARLIE
> She may have become an actress when she grew up. She wanted to.

> JOCK
> Rachel Carpenter. Born Provo, Utah. Mother, Eileen, teacher. Father, James, pianist. Attended—

> CHARLIE
> Don't show off, Jock. Was she ever married?

> JOCK
> Thrice.

> CHARLIE
> And don't imitate my mannerisms. Is she still alive?

> JOCK
> Died nine years ago.

> CHARLIE
> Of course. Of course, dead. How did she die?

Jock doesn't respond.

> CHARLIE
> How?

> JOCK
> Not pleasant.

CHARLIE
Tell me anyway. I want to feel suicidal tonight.

JOCK
In a home for the mentally incapable.

Charlie is silent.

CHARLIE
She was always so brilliant, so quick and intuitive…

LIGHTS UP on Rachel.

RACHEL
When I was playing Helen Keller I needed to understand blindness. It isn't seeing the red insides of your eyelids, it isn't even seeing black. It's like trying to see where you never had eyes at all. Seeing through your knees. No matter how hard you try, there just isn't any *vision* there. *You* didn't laugh when I told you that. My brother laughed. You didn't. That's when I fell in love with you.

LIGHTS DOWN on Rachel.

JOCK
People often outlive their minds these days.

CHARLIE
Yet with the best medical care money can buy, I sit in my room and remember. Remember when passion still lurked behind the lattices of chastity and was more likely to lead to poems than to coitus.

JOCK
Now who's imitating whom?

CHARLIE
I'm an overtold story, Jock. Only tempted because I'm bored. Making excuses because I'm cruel. Lustful because my dim old dong is long past the exercise.

JOCK
Given your lack of heirs, it's debatable whether it was ever up to the exercise. What is it you're tempted by, Charlie?

What could possibly be left in your private catalog of sin? And who's Satan in this story, me or you?

> CHARLIE
> (to himself)
> You *will* do it, because you can. Of all the people in the world, *you* can.

> JOCK
> I'm accustomed to interpreting your half of the conversation, yet even I get confused when you turn cryptic.

> CHARLIE
> I'm going back.

Jock nods, as though expecting this. With a small, graceful gesture of his hand, LIGHTS COME UP Down Left on THIEF, the time-travel device. It can be as elaborate as budgets allow, yet should remain simple in its most basic design: a computer with a halo-like headpiece attached by a cable.

> CHARLIE
> Find me a day.

> JOCK
> For what purpose?

> CHARLIE
> My business.

> JOCK
> Without knowing your purpose, how can I find you a day?

> CHARLIE
> (pause)
> I'm going to be with her. To have her, if I can.

An ALARM sounds. Jock's voice is now different, more mechanized.

> JOCK
> Warning! Warning! Illegal use of THIEF for alteration of the present by manipulation of the past!

The video screen activates at the warning. An antiseptic looking CLINICIAN wearing a labcoat and glasses appears.

CLINICIAN
THIEF—Temporal Hermeneutic Insertion into the Everwhen Field—returns us to the past in the only way possible: within the human mind. Our consciousness travels back in time and subverts—or hacks, if you will—the mind of someone alive and present at the event of our choosing. This person becomes our temporary host in ages past. When our consciousness returns to the present, the host will have no memory of what transpired during our stay, therefore it is critical that they be "safe"—in no position to commit acts that might alter the present timestream. No confusion nor suspicion must arise—

Frustrated, Charlie angrily presses the remote control, and the image disappears.

CHARLIE
Investigation has found the alteration acceptable.

JOCK
Warning! Warning! Illegal use of THIEF—

CHARLIE
Warning: Clear. Program release: Byzantium.

Jock returns to normal.

JOCK
You're a son of a bitch, Charlie.

CHARLIE
Find me a day. A day when the damage will be least. When I can—

JOCK
(quickly)
Twenty-eight October, 2004.

Charlie strains to recall.

JOCK
Three days after returning from your two years in Sâo Paulo. At the very beginning of the three months that broke Rachel's heart, those three months when you were home but didn't call. Afraid of what your friends would say, because she was eight years younger than you, for Pete's sake.

CHARLIE
What will it do to her, Jock?

JOCK
Any answer would call for speculation. And what difference
would it make to you?

CHARLIE
A difference.

JOCK
I can only give you probabilities, Charlie. This isn't like
when you leapt into the mind of an audience member at
the first performance of Handel's Messiah. The poor soul
whose ears you borrowed never remembered a bit of it
afterward—but he **pretended** he loved it—so the future
was not changed. That was safe, to sit in a hall and listen.
This time, though. This time—speaking only in probabilities, mind you—this will change Rachel's life. Not your
own, of course; your younger self won't remember a thing.
But Rachel **will** remember, and it will turn her from the
path she is meant to take. Perhaps only a little. Perhaps not
importantly. Perhaps just enough for her to hate you a little sooner, or a little more. But too much to be legal, if
you're caught.

CHARLIE
I won't be caught. Not when I've allowed the Attorney
General to use THIEF as an untraceable wiretap. Not when
the President...It's safe enough.

JOCK
For you.

CHARLIE
There's nothing left to me, Jock. No one else. You understand?

LIGHTS UP on Rachel.

RACHEL
I understand perfectly. You don't care how I feel...how I felt.
I loved you three years ago, I loved you two years ago, hell, I
even loved you last year, when you got back from Brazil.

JOCK turns toward Rachel, steps into the scene, and becomes YOUNG CHARLIE.

> YOUNG CHARLIE
> Last…? You were dating Alex last y—

> RACHEL
> I was dating a *boy!* Because when you got back from spending two years in Brazil, you didn't call me. All those letters, all those poems you wrote me, and then for three months you didn't call and I knew that you thought I was just a child, so I fell in love with a boy, and now you hate me for it.

> YOUNG CHARLIE
> I don't hate you.

> RACHEL
> What did I do that was so wrong, Charlie? Why didn't you call?

> YOUNG CHARLIE
> Because…you're…we're—

> RACHEL
> Don't talk about our ages.

> YOUNG CHARLIE
> But it's there, it's important, it's all I could think about, my friends all knew how you felt, how I felt, it made me so…

> RACHEL
> What? Made you so what?

> YOUNG CHARLIE
> (softly)
> Ashamed.

> RACHEL
> That's lovely. My love made you feel ashamed. And in return, you give me scorn? Thank you.

> YOUNG CHARLIE
> It wouldn't make a difference if we were twenty years older, even ten…

RACHEL

You could have had me, Charlie. Three years ago, before you left. After you got back. Even when I was with Alex, all you had to do was try, and I would've been yours. Even just a few moments ago you could have had me! Instead, you told me you're ashamed.

Rachel turns to leave. Young Charlie stops her.

YOUNG CHARLIE

I love you. You're the one I always think about. You're the one I always compare other girls to.

RACHEL

Well, that's something. At least I know you'll always remember.

LIGHTS DOWN on Rachel as she exits. Young Charlie becomes Jock again.

JOCK
(still looking after Rachel)
Of course I remember.
(to Charlie)
You gave me all your memories, Charlie. Your wit, your ego…but not your desire. Some things don't translate well to circuitry. Don't ask me to understand, Charlie. Or approve.

CHARLIE

Is there any way to…to lessen…?

JOCK

That's the bitch of time travel, isn't it? You haven't even gone back, and yet already you've ruined her life. The past, in this sense, is inevitable. Because you **will** go back.

Charlie looks away.
JOCK
Even though you know what it'll cost her. What it'll cost you.

Charlie stays silent.

JOCK
Bastard.

Jock walks to the THIEF unit and retrieves the headpiece. Walking over, he places it on Charlie's head. Then very gracefully, he inputs various data into the computer.

            JOCK
You'll wake in twelve hours. Whether you want to return or not.

LIGHTS DOWN SLOWLY over Jock's lines—a SOFT SPOTLIGHT remains on Charlie, lying back, his eyes closed. As the lights fade, a rectangular-shaped spotlight RISES Stage Left: Young Charlie's bed. Jock gestures toward it.

            JOCK
It's 10:20 on a Thursday night. You will enter your young mind when you're standing at the foot of your bed. When the disorientation hits you'll most likely fall. With any luck you'll pitch forward and crack your skull and this little exercise will be over. Look around you, Charlie. Not at the past…

BLACKOUT on all save the bed spotlight.

Scene Two

Jock lies down in the bed spotlight, while Charlie stands beside his bed, leaning on his cane.

CHARLIE
…but the now.

LIGHTS UP. Jock—now YOUNG CHARLIE—lies in bed. His eyes flutter open. He stands, then becomes disoriented.

CHARLIE
And just like that you're young again, Charlie. Flex those muscles. Touch the toes you haven't touched in forty years.

Young Charlie reaches out as if to do so, then stops.

CHARLIE
Look at yourself in the mirror. See the youth you misspent so frivolously.

Young Charlie looks in the mirror. He turns to check his profile, the flatness of his stomach. Charlie stands next to the mirror.

CHARLIE
Curious how many pounds the Brazilian food put on?

Young Charlie begins to flex his muscles.

CHARLIE
Not that many. You were never athletic, even in your twenties.

Young Charlie abandons the flex. Instead, he examines his waistline, rests a hand on his belt.

CHARLIE
It's all there, Charlie. Your virility, your passion, your hunger.

Young Charlie grabs a sweater nearby, looks at it oddly.

CHARLIE
Shocking what we wore in 2004, isn't it?

Young Charlie looks troubled as he contemplates getting dressed. Is he really going to do this? He turns back to the mirror only to see Charlie, who is now Young Charlie's reflection.

> CHARLIE
>
> Don't waste time with regrets, Charlie. Good men resist their own desire when its fulfillment will hurt another person. But you're so powerful you don't need to be good.

Furious with himself, Young Charlie puts on the sweater.

> CHARLIE
>
> It's 10:23, Charlie, and Rachel lives ten minutes away if you run. She goes to sleep at ten. Will you really keep her waiting?

Resolved, Young Charlie exits, hastily.

> CHARLIE
>
> Six blocks away. Up Bailey Boulevard, bulldozed when you built Potter's Field...no, wait, that's another story. One with angels in it. Just head north on Blaine, where Rachel lived, the street that no longer exists because it stood in the way of the highway they named after you. Erasing Rachel's past in your honor.

LIGHTS UP to reveal Rachel's home. Young Charlie steps up to Rachel's door and calls:

> YOUNG CHARLIE
> (softly)
> Rachel?

> CHARLIE
> Louder, Charlie.

> YOUNG CHARLIE
> Rachel?

> CHARLIE
> Faint heart never won fair maid.

> YOUNG CHARLIE
> (loud)
> Rachel!

MRS. CARPENTER enters, nervous at the raised voices. She peers suspiciously out, then is happy once she sees Charlie.

>   MRS. CARPENTER
> Charlie?

>   YOUNG CHARLIE
>   (softly)
> Hi.
>   (louder)
> Hi.

>   MRS. CARPENTER
> Why I heard you were home! Welcome back! It's so won-
> derful to see you.

>   YOUNG CHARLIE
> Thanks…

>   MRS. CARPENTER
> Your folks must be so glad!

>   YOUNG CHARLIE
> Yeah…

>   MRS. CARPENTER
> Rachel goes to bed at ten you know.

>   YOUNG CHARLIE
> She isn't still up?

>   MRS. CARPENTER
> Give me a minute and she will be!
>   (calls offstage)
> Rachel!
>   (to Young Charlie)
> You came back Tuesday, didn't you? I was wondering when
> you'd drop by.

>   YOUNG CHARLIE
> Yeah…I—

RACHEL enters, running at first, then slowing, denying the hurry. In a bathrobe, no shoes, hair messed.

RACHEL
Hi.

Young Charlie tries, but he can't speak.

RACHEL
I heard you were home.

YOUNG CHARLIE
Yeah.

RACHEL
Welcome back.

YOUNG CHARLIE
I didn't mean to wake you.

RACHEL
I wasn't really asleep. The first ten minutes don't count anyway.

YOUNG CHARLIE
I couldn't wait to see you.

RACHEL
You've been home three days. I thought you'd phone.

YOUNG CHARLIE
I hate the telephone. I want to talk to you. I was thinking maybe...

RACHEL
What?

YOUNG CHARLIE
...do you want to walk?

Rachel doesn't even glance at her mother, just turns around for her room.

RACHEL
I'll be right back.

Rachel exits.

YOUNG CHARLIE
I know it's late…

She moves toward Rachel's door, to check on her.

MRS. CARPENTER
That's all right, Charlie, we trust you!

Young Charlie only mouths Old Charlie's words:

CHARLIE
(softly)
Don't. Don't trust me.

Mrs. Carpenter turns back to him, absently.

MRS. CARPENTER
Did you say something?

Young Charlie turns away from her. Rachel arrives, now wearing shoes and wrapping a sweater around her shoulders. She passes Young Charlie heading toward the door and pulls him along in her wake.

MRS. CARPENTER
Don't be too late!

LIGHTS DOWN on the rest of the stage. SPOTLIGHT on Young Charlie and Rachel. Charlie shadows their movements as they walk.

CHARLIE
Is she as you remember, do you think? Does she still have that voice so soft—so soft, that even when she shouts, it gets more whispery?

YOUNG CHARLIE
I missed you.

RACHEL
I missed you too.

CHARLIE
Does she still look the same? Or have decades of regret colored your impressions?

Young Charlie puts his arm around her waist; she doesn't pull away.

RACHEL
You look good. Older. More mature.

YOUNG CHARLIE
Ha. Thanks. You too.

RACHEL
Thanks. 'Bout time.

CHARLIE
I'm curious—why is it you're nervous, Charlie? Just a guess, here…you are not a virgin, but this body does not know that. This body is alert, because it hasn't yet formed the habits of meaningless passion that you know far too well.

Walking downstage right to left, they move into the audience, just across the front of the stage. LIGHTS UP. They look at the empty stage as though arriving at their destination.

RACHEL
The amphitheater? Why here?

YOUNG CHARLIE
You're an actress.

RACHEL
I will be.

Rachel kneels, begins Juliet's death scene.

RACHEL
"O churl! drunk all, and left no friendly drop to help me after?"

She pantomimes pulling Romeo's dagger.

YOUNG CHARLIE
No, wait, do Thisbe!

RACHEL
You mean Pyramus.

Young Charlie nods. Rachel pantomimes the dagger once more.

>   RACHEL
> "Ay, that left pap, where heart doth hop."

As Pyramus, Young Rachel pantomimes stabbing herself, pantomimes the blood spurting, then falls dead, twice. Young Charlie laughs and goes to help her rise.

>   YOUNG CHARLIE
> You're most alive when you're onstage.

>   RACHEL
> So you want me *alive* tonight.

>   YOUNG CHARLIE
> I want you to live forever.

They move Center. Rachel drinks in her surroundings, Young Charlie drinks in Rachel. She takes the stage, pirouetting, and turns toward him. She begins reciting:

>   RACHEL
> "Good pilgrim, you do wrong your hand too much,
> Which mannerly devotion shows in this;
> For saints have hands that pilgrims' hands do touch,
> And palm to palm is holy palmers' kiss."

>   YOUNG CHARLIE
> You'll play Juliet one day.

>   RACHEL
> I know.
>   (suddenly shy)
> When I'm older.

>   YOUNG CHARLIE
> Juliet was thirteen.

>   RACHEL
> Thirteen was older then.

Charlie stands very near, gazing into Rachel's eyes.

>   CHARLIE
>   (to Rachel)
> You should have been born in the Renaissance.

Rachel turns to Young Charlie as though he had spoken.

> YOUNG CHARLIE
> You belong in an age when music was clean and soft and there was no makeup. No one would rival you then.

> RACHEL
> I missed you.

She impulsively kisses Young Charlie, who's momentarily stunned. They both suddenly realize this is the moment. Young Charlie touches her cheek, and she leans into it.

> YOUNG CHARLIE
> You're so beautiful. Even more than I remembered.

He leans in, kisses her lightly, then immediately again. As he pulls away, Rachel grabs him and pulls him to her once more.

> CHARLIE
> Some things…some things can only happen once—

> YOUNG CHARLIE
> (simultaneous)
> Some things…some things can only happen once—

> RACHEL
> Shhh. I'll never forget.

Old Charlie's eyes close in guilt. It's the last thing he wants to hear. LIGHTS BEGIN TO FADE.

> RACHEL
> I love you.

They kiss, tenderly, passionately.

> RACHEL
> All my life I love you.

BLACKOUT.

Scene Three

Charlie lies in bed, underneath the covers. Young Charlie becomes Jock once more. LIGHTS UP. Charlie is bitter, despondent.

    CHARLIE
    (to himself)
Tomorrow…

    JOCK
Welcome back.

Charlie is aghast. He speaks as if to himself, in mounting horror and guilt.

    CHARLIE
Tomorrow, I won't call her. For three months I won't call…and she'll hate me.

Charlie hides his face.

    JOCK
What's wrong?

    CHARLIE
Nothing.

    JOCK
You're crying, Charlie. I've never seen you cry before.

    CHARLIE
Go plug into a million volts, Jock. I had a dream.

    JOCK
What dream?

    CHARLIE
I destroyed her.

    JOCK
No you didn't.

    CHARLIE
It was a selfish thing to do.

JOCK
And you broke your own law to do it. But it didn't hurt her.

CHARLIE
She was a child.

JOCK
No, she wasn't.

CHARLIE
I'm tired. I was asleep. Leave me alone.

JOCK
Charlie, remorse isn't your style.

Charlie pulls the blanket over his head, suddenly petulant and childish.

JOCK
(smiles)
Charlie, let me tell you a bedtime story.

CHARLIE
I'll erase you!

JOCK
Once upon a time, ten years ago, an old woman petitioned
THIEF Community Relations for a day in her past. And
because it was a day with *you,* they called me, as they always
do when your name comes up. She only wanted to visit,
you see, only wanted to relive a good day. Imagine my surprise, Charlie. I didn't know you ever had good days.

Charlie pulls the blanket down, stares at Jock.

JOCK
And in fact, there *were* no good days, none as good as she
thought. Only anticipation and disappointment. That's all
you ever gave anyone, Charlie. Anticipation and disappointment.

CHARLIE
No…

JOCK

And so I created a day for her, Charlie. Only instead of a day of disappointment, or promises she knew would never be fulfilled, I gave her a day of answers. I gave her a night of answers, Charlie.

CHARLIE

You couldn't have known I'd do this. You couldn't have known it ten years ago.

JOCK

It's all right, Charlie, play along with me. You're dreaming anyway, aren't you?

Charlie is suddenly somber.

JOCK

And so an old woman went back into a young girl's body on twenty-eight October 2004, and the young girl never knew what had happened. So it didn't change her life. Don't you see?

CHARLIE

It's a lie.

JOCK

No, it isn't. I can't lie, Charlie. You programmed me not to. Do you think I would have let you go back and **harm** her? You don't have an override code that could make me.

CHARLIE

She was the same. She was as I remembered her.

JOCK

Her body was.

CHARLIE

She hadn't changed.

JOCK

She was dying in an institution…

CHARLIE

She wasn't an old woman…!

JOCK
…with precious few lucid moments left…

CHARLIE
She was a girl…!

JOCK
…surrounded by yellow walls and pale gray sheets and curtains.

CHARLIE
…young and vibrant and *alive*…

JOCK
A young Rachel trapped within a body that could never move again…

CHARLIE
She was a *girl,* Jock!

JOCK
I flashed her picture on the screen this morning, Charlie. To make you remember her…today.

Awareness dawns. Beat.

JOCK
Remember. What was she like, Charlie?

CHARLIE
I put my hand on her cheek. She leaned into it. A woman does that, not a girl.

JOCK
(nods)
I waited ten years for you to get the idea yourself.

CHARLIE
And what she said…"All my life I love you." Not "I *will*…"

JOCK
I had to hurry.

CHARLIE
Why now?

JOCK
Because you're dying, Charlie. Despite all the press releases. Time is running out. You had to go back, today. Because, you see, you already had.

CHARLIE
You couldn't know…

JOCK
I know you pretty well, Charlie. I knew that you'd be enough of a bastard to go back. And enough of a human being to do it right when you got there. She came back happy, Charlie.

CHARLIE
So…it was a lie. The whole night…was all a lie. I wasn't with Rachel, the Rachel I knew, any more than she was with me. The me that…

Charlie stops, as though the anger he looked for wasn't there.

JOCK
Are you angry?

CHARLIE
(shakes his head)
No. A dead woman has given me a gift. And taken the one I offered.

JOCK
Time for sleep, Charlie. Go to sleep again. I just wanted you to know that there's no reason to feel any remorse for it. No reason to feel anything bad at all. There are some things in this world so pure we cannot ruin them, despite our best intentions. Or our worst.

Charlie pulls the covers tight around his neck and closes his eyes; the petulance of earlier in the scene is now purely childlike in its innocence. LIGHTS BEGIN TO FADE. Jock stands at the head of Charlie's bed and begins to recite:

JOCK
"O chestnut tree, great-rooted blossomer,
Are you the leaf, the blossom, or the bole?
O body swayed to music, O brightening glance,
How can we know the dancer from the dance?"

Jock tenderly strokes the old man's hair away from his forehead.

BLACKOUT.

THE END

LIFELOOP

a one-act play by
Aaron Johnston
based upon the short story by
Orson Scott Card

Dedication

To Lauren,
whose affections are always genuine
and whose love is never staged.

Cast of Characters

ARRAN HANDULLY—woman, approximately 25 years old

FELICE—Arran's best friend and confidant

HAMILTON—Arran's former lover

TRUIFF—woman, mid 40s

TECHNICIAN—quick and dutiful

Felice reclines on the sofa reading a gossip magazine. Confetti, dirty glasses, and other items lay scattered around the room—the remnants of a raucous party.

> FELICE
> Did you see this? Julia Roberts died.

> ARRAN
> (offstage)
> Who?

> FELICE
> Julia Roberts. The actress.

> ARRAN
> You mean this Julia Roberts?

Arran enters and makes her best Julia Roberts grin.

> FELICE
> Rude.

> ARRAN
> (exiting)
> She was old.

> FELICE
> She was eighty-two.

> ARRAN
> That's old.

> FELICE
> She acted in such film classics as *Pretty Woman, Steel Magnolias, The Pelican Brief, Armed and Dangerous, Monkey Trouble,* and *Shazbot the Female Android.*

Arran enters and she and Felice do a synchronized Shazbot move.

> FELICE AND ARRAN
> SHAZBOT!

> ARRAN
> Now there's a classic.

FELICE
Get this. Because of the increased popularity in pseudo-reality programs known as Lifeloops, Ms. Roberts was considered by many to be the last of the great film actresses.

ARRAN
Pseudo-reality. What's that supposed to mean?

FELICE
That Lifeloops are fake.

ARRAN
Fake?

FELICE
And that people in Lifeloops are bad actors.

ARRAN
That's ridiculous. Of course they're real.

FELICE
Most people would disagree.

ARRAN
Most people are idiots. Last of the great film actresses my ass.

Arran exits to the bathroom.

FELICE
Why does that upset you?

ARRAN
I'm not upset.

FELICE
You sound upset.

ARRAN
You shouldn't read that trash.

FELICE
It's your magazine.

Arran enters with a bottle of nail polish.

> ARRAN

Lies. All of it. I wouldn't be surprised if Julia Roberts was alive and well, doing cartwheels somewhere.

> FELICE

There's photos of the funeral.

> ARRAN

Photos can be doctored.

> FELICE

The woman was in her eighties. She was old. You said so yourself.

> ARRAN

It's bad journalism. Even if it's true.

> FELICE

You're just miffed because they took a jab at Lifeloops.

Arran frowns as if to say "Puh-lease."

> FELICE

Admit it. You like Lifeloops, and you're annoyed they don't.

> ARRAN

They're entitled to their wrong opinion.

> FELICE

Arran, come on. You can't tell me you really believe the loops are real? You're joking, right?

Pause.

> ARRAN

Put on some boiling water, will you?

> FELICE

You're avoiding my question.

> ARRAN

I'm hungry. And no, they're not actors. They're real people. It's life. Lifeloop. Get it?

FELICE
You don't detect even a hint of theatrics?

ARRAN
People aren't stupid, Felice.

FELICE
No, they're idiots, remember?

Felice exits.

ARRAN
Viewers. Viewers aren't stupid. They can tell what's real and what's fake. The pasta's on the shelf above the stove.

Felice enters with pasta.

FELICE
But maybe they're just really good actors. Don't you think a really good actor can fake being real?

ARRAN
Will you drop it?

FELICE
I mean, if I was an actor—a really talented actor—honed my craft, as they call it, walked the walk, etc.—Don't you think I could fake being real? Isn't that what a good actor is? Someone who's acting, but you can't tell they're acting.

ARRAN
I wouldn't know.

FELICE
Think about the loops. Everything about these people, except for their performance, is fake. I mean, take Brock Singleton for example. Who has a name like Brock? Don't you think that's fake? Even the guy's name is fake.

ARRAN
I know three Brocks, Felice.

FELICE
Are you sure that's their real name?

Arran throws her a look.

> FELICE
> I'm just saying.

She exits with the pasta. We hear it hitting the pot, and she enters.

> FELICE
> OK. Let's assume Brock is his real name. Go with me on this. Brock Singleton. Handsome. Debonair. Charming. Lives in this loft apartment in Manhattan that's got about, I don't know, four thousand square feet. His wardrobe is nothing but Armani and Posh Tucor. He's got a Jackson Pollack hanging over his weight-lifting equipment. He gets laid every night by a different super model, and the man doesn't ever leave his house.

> ARRAN
> So?

> FELICE
> So? Doesn't that strike you as odd?

> ARRAN
> What's odd? A handsome guy in New York who gets laid all the time. Who wouldn't want to watch that?

> FELICE
> Exactly. That's exactly my point. It's too perfect. It's too staged. Guys like that don't exist. It's a fantasy. He's an actor.

> ARRAN
> He's an attorney.

> FELICE
> Who never goes to work?

> ARRAN
> So he works at home.

> FELICE
> He's an actor who lives in an apartment with a hidden camera in every corner, and he gets paid to act like an attorney.

ARRAN

Lifeloops are continuous, Felice. Who would memorize a 24-hour script? It's nonsense.

FELICE

So they improvise.

ARRAN

For twelve days? Each episode is twelve days. Nonstop.

FELICE

OK. What about these women he's always bumping? How does he meet them if he never leaves the house?

ARRAN

I don't know.

FELICE

Somebody has to be sending them to him.

ARRAN

I'm guessing there are plenty of women who watch the show who would love to get in his pants.

FELICE

Aha. Aha. But that's just it. They aren't.

ARRAN

Aren't what?

FELICE

They aren't women who watch the show. They never say, "Oh, Brock, I just love your show." Or, "Oh, Brock, that last episode was amazing." Or "Oh, Brock can I have your auto-graph?" They don't say that. It's always, "Brock, don't you remember me? I was in your third-grade class. Here, take my clothes off." They all know him already. They're phonies. All of them.

ARRAN

You're jealous.

FELICE

Excuse me?

ARRAN
Jealous.

FELICE
Of what?

ARRAN
Brock's women.

Felice makes a sounds as if to say, "Whatever."

ARRAN
You are.

Felice reaches for the toenail polish.

FELICE
Give me that.

Arran holds on to it.

ARRAN
Admit it.

FELICE
I'd like to polish my toenails please.

ARRAN
Who's changing the subject now?

Felice reaches for the bottle again.

ARRAN
Get your own bottle.

FELICE
This is your apartment, not mine.

ARRAN
There's another one in my room if you're so desperate.

Felice goes.

FELICE
Jealous my butt.
> (yelling from offstage)
Where?

ARRAN
On the nightstand.

Felice enters holding a used condom wrapper.

FELICE
Well well well.

ARRAN
What?

FELICE
What is this?

Arran looks then goes back to painting.

FELICE
I'm tired, you said. I'm going to bed early, you said.

ARRAN
I was tired.

FELICE
We throw you this big party, and you sneak off—

ARRAN
I didn't sneak off.

FELICE
You sneak off to your bedroom and get it on with someone while the rest of us are still in here?

ARRAN
That's from a few days ago.

FELICE
Bull. We cleaned your room yesterday.

ARRAN
Well, not thoroughly enough apparently.

FELICE
Who was it?

ARRAN
Will you check the pasta, please?

FELICE
Who was it?

ARRAN
None of your business.

FELICE
You know, you are one twisted little pervert to have the audacity—

ARRAN
I'll do it myself.

Arran goes to the kitchen.

FELICE
To have the audacity to get it on not twenty feet from your own birthday party.

ARRAN
Please. Just stop.

FELICE
You're telling me who it was.

ARRAN
Don't you think you would have heard something?

FELICE
From you? The snake? The seductress? I don't need to have heard anything.

Arran enters.

FELICE
I got the proof right here. Or have you found another use for these I don't know about.

ARRAN
OK, who's the pervert now?

FELICE
Who was it? Richard?

ARRAN
Richard was in here with you.

FELICE
Right. And so was…Phillip, Todd, Jackson, and that Persian guy.

ARRAN
Sching Sching.

FELICE
Right, Sching Sching. I can't believe this. You were in your room last night doing the nasty while I was in here playing Charades with Sching Sching.

ARRAN
You invited him.

FELICE
Who was it then?

ARRAN
Read your magazine.

FELICE
Carlton?

ARRAN
No.

FELICE
Gunther?

ARRAN

Nein.

FELICE

Stuart?

ARRAN

No.

FELICE

Felipe?

ARRAN

No.

FELICE

Donner?

ARRAN

No. Nor Blitzen. Nor Rudolph.

FELICE

Peter?

ARRAN

He wishes.

FELICE

Benjamin?

ARRAN

He died in a plane crash, remember?

FELICE

Oh right.

ARRAN

And thanks for bringing up such a painful memory.

FELICE

Anthony?

ARRAN

No.

FELICE
Frederick?

ARRAN
The conqueror? No.

FELICE
That French guy? What's his name—

ARRAN
Will you stop guessing. I'm not telling you.

FELICE
Hamilton?

Arran looks away.

FELICE
Hamilton. It was Hamilton. I knew it.

ARRAN
It wasn't Hamilton.

FELICE
You paused when I said Hamilton. I know when you're lying.

ARRAN
It wasn't Hamilton.

FELICE
No?

ARRAN
No.

FELICE
But you wish it was Hamilton?

ARRAN
Can we talk about something else please?

FELICE
Arran, you haven't seen Ham in over a year. He's moved on by now.

ARRAN
I'm hungry. You?

She exits.

FELICE
Arran, you've got to accept that Ham's not coming back.
It's over.
(pause)
Are you listening to me? He's not coming back.

ARRAN
(offstage)
Alfredo or marinara?

FELICE
I'm not trying to hurt your feelings, Arran. I'm telling you
this because you're my friend and I want you to be happy.

ARRAN
(offstage)
Marinara. The alfredo smells funny.

FELICE
Ham made a choice. You need to just forget he ever existed.

Quiet sobs from the kitchen. Felice goes to her.

FELICE
You poor thing.

Felice brings a crying Arran to the sofa.

FELICE
Listen to me, Arran. Ham was never good enough for you.
He wasn't. He was a phony. He was never honest. Not once.

ARRAN
He told me he loved me.

FELICE
If he meant it, he wouldn't have left. War or no war.

ARRAN
He didn't have a choice.

FELICE
He enlisted. I call that voluntary.

ARRAN
I drove him away from me.

FELICE
That's not true. You can't blame yourself.

ARRAN
I do.

FELICE
There are plenty of men a thousand times better than Hamilton in this world.

ARRAN
You sound like my mother.

FELICE
Then she was a wise woman.

Arran smiles and wipes her eyes.

FELICE
A smile. You see? That's more like it.

ARRAN
You're my best friend, Felice.

FELICE
Of course I'm your best friend. But who wouldn't want to be friends with Arran Handully, the sweetest, sexiest woman in this city. Now, come on. Tell me about this sexual conquest of yours last night.

ARRAN
I'd rather not.

FELICE
Come on. All the juicy details.

ARRAN
Let's just eat.

She gets up. Felice takes her hand and pulls her back.

FELICE
Wait a second. I was here all day yesterday. And after the party I slept here on the couch. How did this Casanova come and go without me knowing?

ARRAN
Forget it, OK?

FELICE
Was he hiding under your bed or something?

ARRAN
No.

FELICE
Your closet?

ARRAN
Will you stop?

FELICE
He snuck in your window?

ARRAN
Look, I'm starving.

FELICE
Ah cha cha. He snuck in your window.

ARRAN
So he snuck in my window, so what?

FELICE
No, I think it's romantic. It's so Romeo-at-the-balcony. I think that's great.

ARRAN
Great. You're happy. I'm hungry. Let's eat.

Felice pulls her back again.

FELICE
Not so fast, Juliet. You still haven't told me who it was.

ARRAN
It was nobody. You don't know him.

FELICE
Try me.

ARRAN
OK. His name was…Charles. This financial clerk I met.

FELICE
You're lying. I can tell when you're lying. Who was it?

ARRAN
Nobody.

FELICE
Why are you keeping this from me? Do you not want me to know?

ARRAN
Of course not. I mean of course I do.

FELICE
Was is one of my old boyfriends or something?

ARRAN
Can't we just forget about it?

FELICE
No, now you've got me worried. You're keeping this from me.

ARRAN
I'm not keeping it—

FELICE
Then tell me!

ARRAN
No!

FELICE
Tell me or—

ARRAN
Or what? You threatening me?

FELICE
You bet I am. You're keeping this from me for a reason and I'm not going anywhere until…Lucas.

ARRAN
Don't be ridiculous.

FELICE
You balled my fiancé.

ARRAN
That's insane.

FELICE
Admit it. You've been doing the funky watoosy WITH MY FIANCÉ!

ARRAN
So what if I have? He wasn't getting anything good from you.

FELICE
(gasps)
How dare you? You two-timing no-good ungrateful—

ARRAN
And for your information, he came crawling to me.

FELICE
That's a lie.

ARRAN
Ask him yourself. Of course he may not be able to speak just yet. He's probably too exhausted from last night.

FELICE
You whore!

Felice SLAPS Arran. Arran gasps, then SLAPS Felice. The two then choke each other and bite each other.

FELICE
I ought to kill you.

ARRAN
Go ahead and try.

Felice goes to the kitchen and returns with a knife.

ARRAN
Put down the knife, Felice.

Felice gives a maniacal little laugh. Arran screams. Felice chases her around the sofa. They stop then run the opposite direction.

ARRAN
You kill me and Lucas will know it was you. He'll tell the police.

FELICE
Not if I kill him first.

ARRAN
You're crazy.

FELICE
Stark raving mad.

They do another lap around the sofa.

ARRAN
Wait. I'm only doing to you what you did to me first.

FELICE
What are you talking about?

ARRAN
Two…three fiancés ago. Spencer Fozolli. You liquored him up and jumped his bones the night before we were supposed to get married. Or have you forgotten?

Felice lowers the knife.

FELICE
You knew about that?

ARRAN
How was I not supposed to know? I was in my room while
the two of you were in here.

FELICE
But I thought you had stepped out for something.

ARRAN
So you admit it then?

FELICE
I admit nothing.

ARRAN
Oh come off it. I know what Spencer sounds like in the heat
of passion. And I know your voice too.

Felice drops the knife then buries her face in her hands, weeping.

FELICE
I'm the whore. I'm the whore.

Arran goes to her.

ARRAN
Come on. Stop it. You're not a whore.

FELICE
I'm twice the whore you'll ever be. Double Whore, that's me.

ARRAN
You're being silly, Felice.

FELICE
Don't call me that. Call me Whore Whore. I deserve it.

ARRAN
Stop it. Come on, stop crying. Here, sit down.

She sits her down.

FELICE
I'm an awful person. A hypocrite.

ARRAN
Shush already.

FELICE
A hypocrite. An evil wretched hypocrite who sleeps with her best friend's fiancé.

ARRAN
Hey, I slept with your fiancé, remember? So we can call it even.

FELICE
Even?

ARRAN
Sure. You slept with mine. I slept with yours. Even.

FELICE
Even Steven?

ARRAN
Even Steven.

FELICE
You mean that?

ARRAN
Course.

They embrace.

FELICE
You're like a sister to me, Arran.

ARRAN
Don't be so melodramatic, OK? This isn't a soap opera, you know?

Felice laughs while wiping her tears.

FELICE

It could be. Listen to us.
(pause)
You don't hate me for sleeping with Spencer?

ARRAN

Spencer smelt of old onions. My life would have been hell
if I'd married Spencer.
(pause)
And you don't hate me for sleeping with Lucas?

FELICE

His mother's a thorn. I was thinking about breaking it off
anyway.

Pause.

ARRAN

You know, you probably saved me a lot of heartache by
sleeping with Spencer.

FELICE

If you hadn't slept with Lucas, I don't know if I would have
had the courage to break it off.

Pause.

FELICE

Thank you.

ARRAN

No. Thank you.

They embrace again.

ARRAN

The pasta!

Arran bolts to the kitchen.

ARRAN
(offstage)
Crapola.

A knock at the door.

> ARRAN
> (offstage)
> Can you get that?

Felice opens the door. Hamilton is there holding a pizza box.

> FELICE
> Hamilton.

> HAMILTON
> Hello, Felice. Is Arran in?

> ARRAN
> Who is it, Felice?

> FELICE
> Come in. Come in.

Ham enters.

> ARRAN
> The pasta's all runny. It over—

Arran enters carrying a pot. She sees Hamilton and freezes.

> HAMILTON
> Hello, Arran.

> ARRAN
> Hamilton.

Pause.

> HAMILTON
> I guess I should have called first. I brought some pizza, but
> I see you've got dinner already. Maybe I should come back
> some other time when—

Felice grabs his arm.

> FELICE
> No. Pizza's perfect. Right, Arran?

> ARRAN

Right.

Pause.

> FELICE

Well then. I'll just take this back to the kitchen.

Felice takes the pot and exits. Pause.

> HAMILTON

So, how are you? You look great.

> ARRAN

I thought you were in Nigeria.

> HAMILTON

Nigeria? Right.

Felice enters.

> FELICE

Gosh, would you look at the time? You know, I just remembered I put a casserole on at my place…yesterday. I better go see if it's done. Hate to fly off like this but—

She grabs her sleeping bag.

> FELICE

It was nice seeing you, Ham. Bye.

She moves to the door and mouths to Arran "Call me." She exits. Pause.

> HAMILTON

I know you like pineapple and ham, so—

> ARRAN

Especially ham.

She looks at him longingly.

> HAMILTON

Right. Listen, Arran—

ARRAN
You didn't come over here to eat pizza, did you?

HAMILTON
No. I'm not even hungry really.

ARRAN
Me neither. Not for food anyway.

HAMILTON
Look, Arran, I…

ARRAN
…didn't go to Nigeria. That's what you're going to say, isn't it? That you never went to Nigeria. That is was all a lie to get rid of me? No. Don't tell me. I don't want to know.

HAMILTON
Felice looks good. She hasn't changed.

ARRAN
Always the faithful friend.

HAMILTON
And you to her.

ARRAN
I do what I can.

Pause.

ARRAN	HAMILTON
Hamilton—	Look, Arran—

They laugh.

ARRAN
Go ahead.

HAMILTON
I just wanted to say that—well I'm not sure how to say this but—I just wanted to say that I'm sorry about, you know, how things turned out last time.

>ARRAN
> I thought you loved me, Ham.

>HAMILTON
> I did. I mean I do. I always have.

>ARRAN
> Then I'm confused.

>HAMILTON
> They wouldn't let me see you.

>ARRAN
> Are there invisible guardians blocking my door that I don't know about?

Pause.

>HAMILTON
> No.

>ARRAN
> Then I'm confused.
>> (pause)
> Was it someone else, Ham? Another girl?

Ham looks to the door, pauses, then nods. Arran fights back the tears.

>ARRAN
> Who?

>HAMILTON
> Megan.

>ARRAN
> My sister? You left me for my own sister?

>HAMILTON
> Arran, I—

>ARRAN
> Get out.

HAMILTON
Listen to me.

ARRAN
Get out of my house.

HAMILTON
Wait—

ARRAN
(letting the tears come)
I loved you, Hamilton. I loved you and I trusted you. You said I was your light, Ham. Remember that? You said, "Arran you're my light, and only when I'm near you do I really exist." What a bunch of hogwash. What a truckload of malarkey. You backed it up and dumped it right in my lap. I must be the stupidest girl on the planet.

HAMILTON
Stop. I didn't do it, alright? Just stop.

ARRAN
What?

HAMILTON
I didn't do it. I didn't sleep with Megan.

ARRAN
But you just said—

HAMILTON
I know what I said, but I didn't do it, alright? I was making it up.

ARRAN
Making it up?

HAMILTON
I was making it up.

ARRAN
Why would you make that up?

HAMILTON
I lost you once Arran. I'm not going to again.

ARRAN
Are you only saying what I want to hear, Ham? How do I
know you're not only saying what I want to hear?

HAMILTON
You don't. Look, Arran, when I said you were my light, I
meant it. I still do.

Pause.

ARRAN
Did you find what you were looking for?

HAMILTON
Looking for?

ARRAN
In Nigeria. When you left for Nigeria, you said you had to
do something important with your life. That living with
me was turning you into a lovesick shadow.

HAMILTON
I said that?

ARRAN
You were making that up too?

HAMILTON
Lovesick shadow. Well, you see, that was true enough, but
I've discovered that shadows only exist where there is light.

ARRAN
And you've come back to that light, have you?

HAMILTON
Like a moth to a flame.

They kiss.

ARRAN
That was nice.

>   HAMILTON
> I thought so too.
>   (looking into her eyes)
> There's no woman in the world worth loving with you around.

Arran pulls away.

>   ARRAN
> Then why haven't you come back before?

>   HAMILTON
> I wanted to. More than anything.

>   ARRAN
> You mean that?

>   HAMILTON
> Do I sound unconvincing?

No. They kiss again. When they part, Arran begins unbuttoning his shirt. Hamilton stops her.

>   HAMILTON
> No. Not here.

>   ARRAN
> OK.

She takes his hand and leads him toward the bedroom.

>   HAMILTON
> No. I mean not here, in your apartment.

>   ARRAN
> Why?

>   HAMILTON
> Let's go somewhere else. My place. Anyplace. Let's just get
> out of here.

Arran pulls her hand away.

>   ARRAN
> My apartment isn't good enough for you?

HAMILTON
That's not what I meant.

ARRAN
That's what it sounded like to me.

HAMILTON
No, I just meant—

ARRAN
Well, I'm sorry my home is so shabby to you. My father isn't a corporate big-shot like yours. We po' folk can only afford shanty towns like this one. If you're looking for an uptown girl, I'm afraid you've come to the wrong—

HAMILTON
Stop! OK? Cut the act!

ARRAN
What?

HAMILTON
The phony Arran Handully character you're wearing for fun and profit! I know you, Arran, and I'm telling you— I'm telling you, not some actor, me—I'm telling you that I love you! Not for the audiences! Not for the loops! For you—I love you!

ARRAN
Not for the loop?

HAMILTON
I said not for the loop! All these stupid affairs, all the phony relationships. Haven't you had enough?

ARRAN
Enough? This is life, and I'll never have enough of life.

HAMILTON
If this is life, I'm the Easter Bunny.

ARRAN
Ham, you're talking nonsense.

HAMILTON
Do you know what life is, Arran? Life is playing loop after loop after loop, as I've done, screwing every actress who can raise a fee, all so I can make enough money to buy the luxuries of life.

ARRAN
Hamilton, you're frightening me.

HAMILTON
And then one day I realized, all that stuff doesn't amount to squat. Life was so utterly meaningless, just a succession of high-paid tarts!

Arran squeezes out some tears.

ARRAN
Are you calling me a tart?

She throws herself on the sofa. He sits beside her and takes her in his arms.

HAMILTON
You? No. Never you.

ARRAN
What can I think with you coming here and accusing me of being a phony?

HAMILTON
You're not a phony. Every time you told me you loved me, I knew it was true.

ARRAN
Of course it was true.

They kiss again.

ARRAN
Why are you—why are you crying?

HAMILTON
For us, I guess.

ARRAN
Why? What do we have to cry over?

HAMILTON
Lost time.

ARRAN
I don't know about you, but my time has been pretty full.

She laughs. He doesn't.

HAMILTON
We were right for each other, Arran. Not just as a team of actors, but as people. I've looked at the old loops. When we were with other people, we were as phony as no-talent beginners.

ARRAN
I don't agree with your assessment of our past.

HAMILTON
But when we were together we looked real. You know why? Because we weren't acting. We were real. When we told each other we loved each other it was true. We sincerely enjoyed each other's company.

ARRAN
I wish I were enjoying your company now. Telling me I'm a phony and that I have no talent.

He laughs.

HAMILTON
Of course you have talent, and so have I. And money and fame, and everything money can buy. Even friends. But tell me, Arran, how long has it been since you really loved anybody?

ARRAN
I don't think I've ever really loved anybody.

HAMILTON
That's not true, you loved me. A long time ago, you loved me.

ARRAN
Perhaps. But what does that have to do with now?

> HAMILTON
> (concerned)
> Don't you love me now?

> ARRAN
> Love you now? You're just another pair of eager gonads.

Ham looks hurt. He gets up from the sofa and moves for the door.

> ARRAN
> What are you doing?

> HAMILTON
> Leaving.

> ARRAN
> Leaving? Now? No, you can't go.

> HAMILTON
> I was wrong. I'm sorry. I've embarrassed myself.

Arran checks her watch.

> ARRAN
> No, no, Ham, don't leave. I haven't seen you in so long.

> HAMILTON
> You've never seen me. Or you wouldn't have said what you just did.

> ARRAN
> I'm sorry I said it. Forgive me. I didn't mean it.

> HAMILTON
> You just want me to stay so I won't ruin your stupid scene.

She throws herself back onto the sofa, weeping.

> ARRAN
> That's right. Leave me now when I want you so much.

Pause.

HAMILTON
You mean that?

ARRAN
(through tears)
Mmmm-hmmm.

HAMILTON
Not as an actress, Arran, please. As yourself. Do you love me?

ARRAN
Like nothing I've ever loved before. Why have you stayed
away so long?
(pause)
Look in my eyes, Ham. What do I have to say to convince you?

He gets close to her face and stares at her eyes.

HAMILTON
You're either a better actress than I thought or you do
mean that.

She grabs his face and kisses him.

HAMILTON
Marry me.

ARRAN
Do you mean it?

HAMILTON
Marry me. I want you with me always.

ARRAN
Always is a long time.

HAMILTON
Screw the loops. We've both got enough money. We don't
have to let them control our lives ever again.

Pause. She moves away from him.

ARRAN
I won't marry you.

HAMILTON

Please, Arran. Don't you see that I love you? Do you think any of these phonies who pay to sleep with you will ever feel one shred of real emotion toward you? To them you're just a chance to make a name for themselves.

ARRAN

Is that what I am to you? A no-talent, phony prostitute?

HAMILTON

What? No. Arran, I'm being serious. I'm not in character.

ARRAN

You're a liar.

HAMILTON

Why would I lie? Haven't I made it plain to you that I'm telling the truth? That I'm not acting?

ARRAN

(snidely)

Not acting? Not acting? Well, as long as we're being honest about things, and throwing away both pretense and art, I'll play it your way. Do you know what I think of you? I think this is the cheapest, dirtiest trick I've ever seen. Coming here like this, doing everything you could to lead me into thinking you loved me, when all the time you were just exploiting me. Worse than all the others! You're the worst.

HAMILTON

I'd never exploit you.

ARRAN

Marry me? Ha! Marry me, says you, and then what? What if this poor little girl actually did marry you? What would you do? Force me to stay in this flat forever? Keep away all my other friends, all my other—yes, even my lovers, you'd make me give them all up! Hundreds of men love me, but you, Hamilton, you want to own me forever, exclusively! What a coup that would be, wouldn't it? No one would ever get to look at my body again except you. And you say you don't want to exploit me.

Hamilton goes to her, but she pushes him away.

    ARRAN
Stay away from me.

    HAMILTON
Arran, you don't mean that.

    ARRAN
I have never meant anything so thoroughly in my life.

    HAMILTON
Arran, please. Nothing else in my life means anything anymore. I'm finished. I'm sick of it all. If you mean what you
say—if it's not an act—I don't think I can handle that.

    ARRAN
What is that supposed to mean, Ham? Are you on a ledge or
something? Am I supposed to talk you down from the ledge?
    (mockingly)
Don't jump, Ham. Don't jump. Well if suicide is on your
to-do list, pal, don't let me stop you. Considering the way
you've used me today, I say you deserve it.

*Pause. Ham turns and goes. He couldn't look more crestfallen. Once he's gone,
Arran throws herself on the sofa, weeping.*

    ARRAN
Wait, Hamilton. Don't go. Don't go, Hamilton. I love you.
What have I done? Please come back. Forgive me, Ham,
forgive me.

A loud BUZZER sounds. TRUIFF and TECHNICIAN enter.

    TRUIFF
And we're clear.

Arran immediately stops crying.

    ARRAN
What the hell was that all about?

    TRUIFF
Wow! What an episode.

ARRAN
I'm starving.

TRUIFF
(to Technician)
Bring Ms. Handully a sandwich.

ARRAN
No meat, no mustard, no mayo.

TRUIFF
No meat, no mustard, no mayo.

The technician scurries off.

TRUIFF
Oh that was beautiful, Arran. You should have seen me in
the sound booth. Tears. Real tears. Buckets. Beautiful.

ARRAN
(fuming)
Where is Felice? She really choked me.

TRUIFF
I know. She didn't mean it.

ARRAN
I couldn't breathe.

TRUIFF
You poor thing.

ARRAN
Poor thing? I want her off the show.

TRUIFF
She was balling her eyes out in the booth, Arran. She didn't
mean it. I swear.

ARRAN
Well, I choked her back. The troll.

TRUIFF
I know. I think that was partially why she was crying.

ARRAN

And why was she talking about the loops? Was she trying to destroy me? Saying we're actors?

TRUIFF

Ratings are slipping. People are starting to think you are actors. By addressing the issue head-on, we put their minds at ease.

ARRAN
(sarcastically)

Bloody brilliant.

The technician returns with a sandwich. He hands it to Arran.

ARRAN

RYE. RYE. I eat rye, you git. This is wheat.

She pushes it in his face.

TRUIFF
(to the technician)

A rye sandwich.

He scoops up the wheat sandwich and goes.

ARRAN

And what the was Hamilton doing? Talking about breaking character? What was that all about?

TRUIFF

He was supposed to stick with the sleeping-with-your-sister story. I don't know why he dropped it. I'll call his agent. Very unprofessional.

ARRAN
(suddenly very happy)

Could you have him meet me in the green room? I'm dying to talk to him.

TRUIFF

I would, Love, but he didn't return to the booth. He was peeling away when the buzzer sounded.

Arran's smile vanishes.

>   ARRAN
> He didn't go to the booth?

>   TRUIFF
> Walked right by me. Crying too. I'm telling you, it was the
> best show ever, Arran. Hands down.

>   ARRAN
> He was crying?

>   TRUIFF
> The entire crew was crying. You were marvelous. Pure genius.

Arran sits on the couch. Numb.

>   TRUIFF
> It's true what he said, you know? His best acting was always
> with you. I was afraid he didn't have it in him anymore. He
> hasn't taken a gig since he left the show last time.

>   ARRAN
> He quit?

>   TRUIFF
> Turned down every loop offered him. He kept begging to
> get on with you, of course, but the time wasn't right. Wow,
> what an episode.

>   ARRAN
> I have to talk to him.

>   TRUIFF
> Don't be silly, darling. We're on again in thirty seconds.

>   ARRAN
> He thinks I don't love him.

>   TRUIFF
> And speaking of guest appearances, Brock Singleton's show
> was cancelled. He's available. He'll show up in a day or two
> and break up things between you and Sching Sching.

>   ARRAN
> Sching Sching?

TRUIFF
In the next episode. We're calling it "Arran's fling with Sching Sching." Catchy, huh?

ARRAN
I don't love Sching Sching.

TRUIFF
Not yet, tigress. And remember, it's a double feature. Twenty-four days. Try and think of a reason why you'd need an attorney. That's how we'll introduce Brock. But don't mention legal terms. The man's got rocks for brains.

TRUIFF blows Arran a kiss and exits. The technician enters with the sandwich, but Arran pushes it away, uninterested. Then, as if speaking to an unseen camera:

TECHNICIAN
We're on in five…four…three…

He exits. Arran sits zombie-like on the couch. Void of emotion. Void of life. At one, when the show is set to begin, lights out.

THE END

AFTERWORD

by Aaron Johnston

As far as I can tell, with the exception of a few campy comedies like *Little Shop of Horrors,* science fiction is mostly absent from modern theater. And frankly that's a shame, especially for someone like me who loves both worlds.

I can only speculate why this is the case, but one reason might be the notion that since most science fiction stories are set in the future, the costumes and sets must look "futuristic."

Well, nothing could be farther from the truth. In fact, from the outset of this production Scott Card made it clear to both our set and costume designers that we would not attempt to guess what the future looks like. Even our best guesses would be wrong, and chances are the end result would look silly.

So we made no attempt to design the fashions of tomorrow. Instead, our actors wore clothes that were fashionable at the time. Sure there was a little spunk to the wardrobe, a subtle nod to what the clothes of the future may look like, but nothing you wouldn't see on the street today.

And with the exception of a few blocks that served as furniture, the set and walls were bare, allowing the audience to use their imagination to decide how the homes of the future would be decorated.

Besides, as any fan of Orson Scott Card can tell you, science fiction stories need not be set in the future at all. "Sepulchre of Songs" is a perfect example. And in truth, "Lifeloop" is another. All of the science that makes this story possible exists today.

Of course, science—particularly science as it appears in the fiction of Orson Scott Card—is always secondary, if not tertiary, to the story. What really makes these stories engaging are the characters and the incredibly difficult, sometimes painful decisions they're forced to make.

That's why if you whittle away or change some of those scientific elements, the story usually remains intact.

At least that was my hope when I started adapting this story.

"Lifeloop" was first published in October 1978 in *Analog Science Fiction* and later in a collection of stories entitled *Capitol*, which sadly is out of print. The story was later reprinted in *The Worthing Saga*, which I highly recommend.

All of the stories within *The Worthing Saga* take place in a universe in which the drug somec exists. Those who can afford the drug use it to sleep indefinitely, sometimes for centuries at a time, granting themselves near immortality.

I loved the premise of the drug. It fascinated me. But I knew it wasn't necessary for the play. It would only add another dimension to the story and call for more exposition. So I dropped it. I whittled away some of the science.

What I couldn't sacrifice, of course, was the idea of Lifeloops themselves. Everything depended on the audience understanding what a Lifeloop was. In fact, the very crux of the story was Arran having to choose between her successful career as a Lifeloop actor and the one true love of her life, Hamilton. (Sometimes it's more interesting, Scott Card once told me, to force a character to choose between two seemingly good options than between a good and bad one).

So I introduced Felice. Her name in the original story was Doret, but I changed it because I feared Doret might be distracting as a stage name. Felice proved extremely useful as a supporting character in the play because not only was she a vehicle for the exposition—explaining to the audience through her dialogue with Arran exactly what a Lifeloop was—but also the instigator of some serious melodrama. Lifeloops, after all, are "reality soaps" that follow many traditional soap opera conventions.

But the melodrama couldn't be too thick. Viewers still needed to believe that this was real, that what they were watching was reality television, not actors improvising.

For that to work, Scott Card instructed the actors to play their characters, who were actors, as believably as possible. It had to feel real. They couldn't over-act.

This was especially important since I had decided not to reveal to the audience that the play itself was a Lifeloop, that the stage was a stage, that the characters were really actors talking about actors. That twist would be revealed to the audience slowly, clue by clue, as the show progressed and then fully disclosed when the buzzer sounded and Truiff entered, essentially ending the episode.

But I wasn't done. I also had to decide what to do about Hamilton. In the story he kills himself, but only after Arran has been put to sleep with somec and a lot of time has passed.

Since I staged the play in a single setting and in real time, the idea of Hamilton immediately going out and killing himself before the play concluded seemed too melodramatic even by soap opera standards. Plus I didn't want to have to deal with the off-stage sounds of someone taking their own life. It just didn't work.

So he simply leaves. And since Arran is about to begin a double-feature, she won't have a chance to talk to him for a very long time. What Hamilton does to himself during that time is anyone's guess.

When we opened the production, "Lifeloop" was the first of the three one-acts shown. The audience's response that night was not what I had expected. I had expected a few laughs. The show wasn't bust-a-gut funny, I knew, but I thought there were at least a few slightly humorous moments.

No one in the audience agreed. Or if they did, they didn't vocalize it. I was very concerned. The crowd apparently didn't think it was funny.

That night after the performance, I spoke with Scott Card. Someone had suggested changing the order of the one-acts and putting "Lifeloop" second, after "Clap Hands and Sing." I thought this was a good idea and asked if I could sharpen some of the dialogue at the beginning of "Lifeloop." Scott said yes.

For the rest of the evening I racked my brain. Why the quiet reaction? Why the stoned response?

I finally came to this conclusion: the audience didn't know what to expect. They had never been to a science fiction production and didn't realize that laughter was permissible.

Think about it. If you buy tickets to a comedy, you know you're supposed to laugh. You expect to be amused. Your laugh reflex is ready. The same goes for a tragedy. If you buy tickets to a serious drama, you leave the laugh reflex at the door. In fact, even if the tragedy is miserably bad, so bad it's laughable, you don't laugh. That's proper theater etiquette.

So the crowd coming to *Posing As People* didn't know how they were supposed to react. They were more than willing to respond appropriately, I'm sure. They just didn't know what *was* appropriate.

So I knew I needed an immediate laugh. I knew I had to tell the audience right out of the gate that, Hey, it's OK to chuckle during this play. Think of this as a comedy. Sit back and relax and loosen that laugh reflex.

I cut a page and a half of dialogue at the very beginning and Scott and I inserted some physical humor. Because the jokes are mostly visual, you the reader may not see the humor and think my dilemma went unsolved.

But lucky for me, it worked. On the second night, the laughs began. On some nights the laughs were huge. The response was remarkably different.

I can't take credit for ninety percent of those laughs, though. The cast found new and funny ways to breathe life and laughter into the roles.

But don't get me wrong. I don't think of "Lifeloop" as a comedy. For me, it's a tragedy through and through. I simply thought it would be fun to have a few laughs before the sobering conclusion. And when that finally came, when the lights went out and Arran's solemn face disappeared into darkness, the audience knew how to respond. They applauded.

I'd like to think that at that moment, at least, they weren't just being polite.

A SEPULCHRE OF SONGS

a one-act play by
Emily Janice Card
based upon the short story by
Orson Scott Card

Dedication

to my parents,
thank you for everything

Cast of Characters

ELAINE—bright 16 year old

APRIL—nurturing and in charge; head nurse at the Millard County Rest Home

THERAPIST—late 20's to early 30's; easy warmth, self-deprecating

DOUG—another nurse; jocular but responsible

WALLACE BAITY—gruff with an ornery charm; a resident of the rest home

BECKY—mid to late 20's; the woman you bring home for Christmas

Lights go up on a bed stage right. It has hospital white sheets and a utilitarian sort of blanket, and is at a raised, 75 degree angle, so that the occupant of the bed can sit up. There is a stool at the foot of the bed, and a small table and CD player at the head. The right wall has a window. Upstage center, there is also a tall counter, the nurses' station, with a chair behind it, and files scattered on the counter top. There are windows on the wall behind the nurse's station.

ELAINE enters from stage left, carrying a vase of flowers. She is wearing a long black shirt that hangs past her hips, and long black bicycle-type shorts. She is barefoot. She crosses the stage and sets the flowers on the small table by the bed. She explores the stage a little, sits on the counter top of the nurse's station, then skips back to the bed, circles around it, and stops to look out the window on the stage right wall. APRIL enters, and ELAINE joins her at the nurse's station. APRIL hands her a pair of long opaque white stockings. ELAINE crosses to sit on the bed and puts on the stockings. APRIL comes over, and as ELAINE lifts the blanket, APRIL lifts her legs into the bed and, more importantly, into a hole that the audience should not see, so that when ELAINE is covered with the blanket, her legs appear to end at the knee. Then APRIL puts a long white glove on each of ELAINE's arms and tucks them under the blanket as well. In this way, ELAINE's arms and legs are theatrically "missing."

APRIL goes to the nurse's station. THERAPIST enters.

    THERAPIST
I was first assigned to see Elaine at the Millard County Rest Home to get rid of her imaginary friends. I remember April, the head nurse, telling me what to expect.

THERAPIST crosses to the nurse's station. APRIL gives him a file folder.

    APRIL
She's kept these friends long after most children give them up.

    THERAPIST
How old *is* Elaine?

    APRIL
Sixteen.

    THERAPIST
I'm guessing she's the youngest patient here.

    APRIL
By far. She's a ward of the state. When she was five years

old, she survived an oil truck explosion that killed both her parents.

> THERAPIST
> (nodding)
> The explosion that took her arms and legs.

> APRIL
> She doesn't have much more than a torso, so it's upsetting to see this little lump of a body surrounded by too much emptiness on the bed. But Elaine's a doll. She's stubborn, and she insists on being liked.

> THERAPIST
> And do you like her?

> APRIL
> She's my favorite face.

THERAPIST steps into ELAINE's room. Her head is turned away from him as she looks out the window. He crosses in front of her bed to sit on the stool at the corner of her bed.

> THERAPIST
> Hi, Elaine.

> ELAINE
> Oh, hi. You're just in time. I was on my way out.

> THERAPIST
> Where were you going?

> ELAINE
> France. The Louvre called. They need a stand-in while they get the Venus de Milo cleaned. (THERAPIST is flustered, unsure how to respond. ELAINE bursts out laughing) Oh, wow, I'm going to have to break you in.

> THERAPIST
> Darn, and my degree says I'm fully trained.

> ELAINE
> Not at the school of Elaine.

THERAPIST
You're right. I want to learn all about you. And your friends.

ELAINE
Okay. They're imaginary.

THERAPIST
What?

ELAINE
My friends. So you can't meet them or anything.

THERAPIST
Oh. Are you sure? They might like me.

ELAINE
I might like you if you stopped talking craziness.

THERAPIST
So you know your friends aren't real.

ELAINE
Yeah, but I guess you didn't.

THERAPIST
Your file says you've talked about them for years. And you talk *to* them, as well.

ELAINE
Well, sometimes I have to convince Howard not to beat people up.

THERAPIST
Howard's one of your friends?

ELAINE
When I'm pretending. He's this stout little kid with a permanent milk crust around his mouth who really likes to hit things.

THERAPIST
Why does he hit things?

ELAINE

Because when I'm mad, somebody should hit stuff. Talking about him calms me down when I want to say mean things.

THERAPIST

Howard is how you deal with anger.

ELAINE

Exactly! But when I'm in a good mood, I let him be a sweet little goober.

THERAPIST

What about the girl who comes to play with you?

ELAINE

Fuchsia. She only comes inside if I get some new plant or bouquet in my room.

THERAPIST

Why is that?

ELAINE

Because she's three inches high and lives among the flowers.

THERAPIST

If you know these people don't exist, why do you still talk about them?

ELAINE

I know I'm too old for it. But my life gets really boring, and I try to entertain myself.

THERAPIST

Is it entertaining when people think you're serious, and call me in here and make *me* act serious?

ELAINE

I thought it was obvious I was telling stories. I mean, my best friend is a pig made out of ice!

THERAPIST

That's pretty common.

ELAINE
(*taken aback*)

It is?!

THERAPIST

Where do you think porksicles come from?

ELAINE
(*Groans, but she is amused*)

You're not acting serious anymore.

THERAPIST

Nope. Too hard. But we still have half an hour left. Can I hang out in here and pretend I'm still working?

ELAINE

Sure! We can curse and smoke.

THERAPIST

And read comics.

ELAINE

Do you have any?

THERAPIST

I'll bring some next time. Any requests? From you or the pig?

ELAINE

His name is Grunty. And we like <u>The Sandman</u>.

ELAINE bows her head and THERAPIST steps away from the scene, speaking to the audience.

THERAPIST

I continued to see Elaine once a week, not entirely because I liked her so much. Partly because I wondered whether she had been pretending when she told me she knew her friends weren't real. But I felt they did her no harm at all, and destroying that imaginary world would only make her lonelier. She was saner than I would have been, in her place.

The sound of rain begins. THERAPIST crosses to the nurses' station. APRIL sits behind the counter on a tall stool, and DOUG, another nurse, stands in front, leaning on the counter.

DOUG

It's been pouring for days, and we have to keep the patients inside. The mood barometer here reads: Cranky.

APRIL

Elaine doesn't complain much, but it hurts her the worst. She depends so much on those hours outside.

THERAPIST

I've seen her being wheeled in from the yard. She smiles and looks so delighted I almost expect her to start waving at me and bouncing up and down.

APRIL

Her happiness is contagious.

DOUG

Yeah, once she's in her chair, we race down the hall and she yells "Faster, faster!" until we get to the glass doors. Then I slow way down and she sings the *Chariots of Fire* theme till we're outside.

DOUG begins to pantomime the slow wheelchair push as he sings the theme song, until APRIL lovingly pushes him out the door. THERAPIST moves to stand at the entrance to ELAINE's room.

THERAPIST

It rained four weeks, and I nearly lost her.

ELAINE

Raining, raining, raining.

THERAPIST

Don't I know it? I'm leaving puddles wherever I go.

ELAINE

Bad dog.

THERAPIST

I heard you were depressed. I'm supposed to make you happy.

ELAINE

Make it stop raining.

THERAPIST
Do I look like God?

ELAINE
I thought maybe you were in disguise. *I'm* in disguise. I'm really a large Texas armadillo who was granted one wish. I wished to be a human being. But there wasn't enough armadillo to make a full human being, so here I am.
> (*He chuckles; she smiles. Then she turns her head to look out the window*)

I want to go outside.

THERAPIST
You'd get sick.

ELAINE
Not me. I've got a poncho.

THERAPIST
(*walking behind the bed toward the window*)
And later it can catch the drips from your runny nose.

ELAINE
Outer space is like the rain. It sounds like that out there, just a low drizzling sound in the background of everything.

THERAPIST
Not really. There's no sound out there at all.

ELAINE
How do *you* know?

THERAPIST
There's no air. Can't be any sound without air.

ELAINE
(*scornfully*)
Just as I thought. You don't *really* know. You've never *been* there, have you?

THERAPIST
(*leaning against the window sill, facing her*)
Are you trying to pick a fight?

ELAINE
(*starts to answer, catches herself, and nods*)
Damned rain.

THERAPIST
At least you don't have to drive in it. (*He realizes he has taken the banter too far.*) Hey. First clear day I'll take you out driving.

ELAINE
It's hormones.

THERAPIST
What's hormones?

ELAINE
I'm sixteen. It always bothered me when I had to stay in. But I want to scream. My muscles are all bunched up, my stomach is all tight, I want to go outside and *scream*. It's hormones.

THERAPIST
(*sits on the stool*)
What about your friends?

ELAINE
Are you kidding? They're all out there, playing in the rain.

THERAPIST
All of them?

ELAINE
Except Grunty, of course. He'd dissolve.

THERAPIST
And where's Grunty?

ELAINE
(*as if he is the stupidest person on the planet*)
In the freezer.

THERAPIST
Someday the nurses are going to mistake him for ice cream and serve him to the guests.

(*ELAINE nods but does not smile.*)

THERAPIST
Do you want something?

ELAINE
No pills. They make me sleep all the time.

THERAPIST
If I gave you uppers, it would make you climb the walls.

ELAINE
Neat trick.

THERAPIST
It's that strong. So do you want something to take your mind off the rain and these four ugly walls?

ELAINE
(*shakes her head*)
I'm trying not to sleep.

THERAPIST
Why not?

ELAINE
(*again she shakes her head*)
Can't let myself sleep too much.

THERAPIST
Why not?

ELAINE
(*sternly*)
Because I might not wake up.

THERAPIST
Elaine, that's not—

ELAINE
Time out. All done. Don't you have a hot date to get to?

THERAPIST
It's true, I am seeing other people today. My whole job is just one hot date after another.

ELAINE
What about your girlfriend?

THERAPIST
What girlfriend?

ELAINE
I met that woman once . . . Becky, right? We were in the yard and she came by to pick you up for lunch or something.

THERAPIST
I forgot about that. Becky and I used to date, but now we're just friends. Actually, she's the closest I come to having my own therapist.

ELAINE
So you call your patients your dates and your girlfriend your therapist. You are a very confused man.

THERAPIST
(Laughs) Maybe so. I'll try to figure it out before I see you next week. You take care now. (He is almost out of the room before he turns around.) And Elaine?

ELAINE
Hm?

THERAPIST
You *will* wake up.

Lights dim on ELAINE, and THERAPIST leaves her room to address the audience center stage.

THERAPIST
And then I left, and to tell the truth I didn't think about her much. My job was one of the worst in the state, touring six rest homes in six counties, and visiting each of them every week. I "did therapy" wherever the administrators thought therapy was needed. Weekends I lived alone in a trailer in Piedmont, and I passed the weeks with highways, depressed

people, and sandwiches and motels at state expense.

You don't end up as a state-employed therapist if you had much ability in college. As one kindly brutal professor told me, I wasn't cut out for science. But I was sure I was cut out for the art of therapy. Ever since I comforted my mother during her final year of cancer I believed I had a knack for helping people get straight in their minds. I was everybody's confidant.

So I got over the initial disappointment in my career and made the best of it. Elaine was the best of it.

Lights up on ELAINE again. It is a week later.

> ELAINE
> (*addressing the stool as if THERAPIST were already seated there*)
> Where have you been?

> THERAPIST
> (*crossing into Elaine's room again and sitting on the stool*)
> Locked in a cage suspended over a pond filled with crocodiles. I got out by picking the lock with my teeth. Luckily, the crocodiles weren't hungry. Where have *you* been?

> ELAINE
> I mean it. Don't you keep a schedule?

> THERAPIST
> I'm right on my schedule, Elaine. This is Wednesday. I was here last Wednesday. This year Christmas falls on a Wednesday, and I'll be here on Christmas.

> ELAINE
> It feels like a year.

> THERAPIST
> Only ten months. Till Christmas. Elaine, you aren't being any fun.

> ELAINE
> I can't stand much more.

THERAPIST
I'm sorry.

ELAINE
I'm afraid. At night, and in the daytime, whenever I sleep.
I'm just the right size.

THERAPIST
For what?

ELAINE
What do you mean?

THERAPIST
You said you were just the right size.

ELAINE
I did? Oh, I don't know what I meant. I'm going crazy.
That's what you're here for, isn't it? To keep me sane. It's the
rain. I can't do anything, I can't see anything, and all I can
hear most of the time is the hissing of the rain.

THERAPIST
Like outer space.

ELAINE
(startled)
How did you know?

THERAPIST
You told me.

ELAINE
There isn't any sound in outer space.

THERAPIST
Oh, of course.

ELAINE
There's no air out there.

THERAPIST
I knew that.

ELAINE

The engines. You can hear them all over the ship. It's a drone, all the time. That's just like the rain. Only after a while you can't hear it anymore. It becomes like silence. Anansa told me.

THERAPIST

Who's Anansa?

ELAINE

Oh, you don't want to know.

THERAPIST

I want to know.

ELAINE

I can't make you go away, but I wish you would. When you get nosy.

THERAPIST

It's my job.

ELAINE
(contemptuously)
Job! I see all of you, running around on your healthy legs, doing all your *jobs*.

THERAPIST

It's how we stay alive. I do my best.

ELAINE

Maybe I can get a job, too.

THERAPIST

Maybe.

ELAINE

There's always music.

THERAPIST

There aren't many instruments you can play. That's the way it is.

ELAINE
Don't be stupid.

THERAPIST
Okay. Never again.

ELAINE
I meant that there's always the music. On my job.

THERAPIST
And what job is this?

ELAINE
Wouldn't you like to know?
(*She rolls her eyes mysteriously and turns toward the window.*)

THERAPIST
What kind of job is Anansa going to give you?

ELAINE
(*turning back to him, startled*)
So it's true, then.

THERAPIST
What's true?

ELAINE
It's so frightening. I keep telling myself it's a dream. But it isn't, is it?

THERAPIST
What, Anansa?

ELAINE
You think she's just one of my friends, don't you. But they're not in my dreams, not like this. Anansa—she sings to me. In my sleep.

THERAPIST
Of course.

ELAINE
She's in space, and she sings to me. You wouldn't believe the songs.

THERAPIST
Oh, that reminds me.
(*He reaches into his jacket and pulls out a CD.*)
I got this for you today, when I realized it's been raining for a week and you must be sick of everything. It's Copland.

ELAINE
Thank you.

THERAPIST
You're welcome. Want to hear it?

She nods. He puts it in the CD player by her bed. The music begins. ELAINE closes her eyes and takes the music in, but soon it frustrates and upsets her.

ELAINE
It's not the same.

THERAPIST
You've heard it before?

ELAINE
Turn it off. Turn it *off*!

He turns it off.

THERAPIST
Sorry. Thought you'd like it.

ELAINE
Guilt, nothing but guilt. You always feels guilty, don't you?

THERAPIST
(*cheerfully*)
Pretty nearly always.

ELAINE
I'm sorry. It's just—it's just not the music. Not *the* music. Now that I've heard it, everything is so dark compared to it. Like the rain, all gray and heavy and dim, as if the

composer is trying to see the hills but the rain is always in the way. For a few minutes I thought he was getting it right.

THERAPIST
Anansa's music?

ELAINE
(*Nods.*)
I know you don't believe me. But I hear her when I'm asleep. She tells me that's the only time she can communicate with me. She's out there, in her starship, singing. And at night I hear her.

THERAPIST
Why you?

ELAINE
You mean, Why only me?
(*Laughs.*)
Because of what I am. You told me yourself. Because I can't run around. I live in my imagination. She says that the threads between minds are very thin and hard to hold. But mine she can hold, because I live completely in my mind. She holds on to me. When I go to sleep, I can't escape her now anymore at all.

THERAPIST
Escape? I thought you liked her.

ELAINE
I don't know what I like. I like—I like the music. But Anansa wants me. She wants to have me—she wants to give me a job.

She trembles and closes up. There is a pause, while he thinks of something she seemed willing to talk about.

THERAPIST
What's the singing like?

ELAINE
It's not like anything. She's there in space, and it's black, just the humming of the engines like the sound of rain, and she reaches into the dust out there and draws in the songs.

She reaches out her—out her fingers, or her ears, I don't know; it isn't clear. She reaches out and draws in the dust and the songs and turns them into the music that I hear. It's powerful. She says it's her songs that drive her between the stars.

THERAPIST
Is she alone?

ELAINE
(*Nods.*)
She wants me.

THERAPIST
Wants you. How can she have you, with you here and her out there?

ELAINE
I don't want to talk about it.

THERAPIST
I wish you would. I really wish you'd tell me.

ELAINE
She says—she says that she can take me. She says that if I can learn the songs, she can pull me out of my body and take me there and give me arms and legs and fingers and I can run and dance and—

She breaks down, crying. He reaches to touch her forehead, but she quickly turns her head away. So he pats her belly, the only place she ever permits.

THERAPIST
It's a lovely dream, Elaine.

ELAINE
It's a terrible dream. Don't you see? I'll be like *her.*

THERAPIST
And what's she like?

ELAINE
She's the ship. She's the starship. And she wants me with her, to be the starship with her. And sing our way through space together for thousands and thousands of years.

THERAPIST
It's just a dream. Elaine. You don't have to be afraid of it.

ELAINE
They did it to her. They cut off her arms and legs and put her into the machines.

THERAPIST
But no one's going to put you into a machine.

ELAINE
I want to go outside.

THERAPIST
You can't. It's raining.

ELAINE
Damn the rain.

THERAPIST
I do, every day.

ELAINE
I'm not joking! She pulls me all the time now, even when I'm awake.
(*She gets more and more frantic, rocking her body from side to side.*)
She keeps pulling at me and making me fall asleep, and she sings to me, and I feel her pulling and pulling. If I could just go outside, I could hold on. I feel like I could hold on, if I could just—

THERAPIST
(*already moving toward the door, to get medication*)
Hey, relax. Let me give you a—

ELAINE
No! I don't want to sleep!

APRIL *looks up from her work when she hears* ELAINE *yell.* APRIL *and* THERAPIST *exchange a look before he comes back into* ELAINE's *room.*

THERAPIST
Listen, Elaine. You can't let it get to you like this. It's just the

rain keeping you here. It makes you sleepy, and so you keep dreaming this. But don't fight it. It's a beautiful dream in a way. Why not go with it?

> ELAINE
> (*Terror in her eyes*)
> You don't mean that. You don't want me to go.

> THERAPIST
> No. Of course I don't want you to go anywhere. But you won't, don't you see? It's a dream, floating out there between the stars—

> ELAINE
> She's not floating! She's ramming her way through space so fast it makes me dizzy whenever she shows me.

> THERAPIST
> Then be dizzy. Think of it as your mind finding a way for you to run.

> ELAINE
> You don't understand, Mr. Therapist. I thought you'd understand.

> THERAPIST
> I'm trying to.

> ELAINE
> If I go with her, then I'll be dead.

DOUG enters.

> DOUG
> 'Scuse me for interrupting, but I needed Elaine's vote on afternoon ice cream. Yay or nay, babe?

ELAINE shakes her head and starts to reply, but THERAPIST jumps in.

> THERAPIST
> Is the ice cream at all pig-shaped?

> DOUG
> No, I believe it's shaped like a big bucket of Food Lion vanilla.

THERAPIST
Then Grunty's safe. You can have a guilt-free bowl, Elaine.

ELAINE
(*Smiles a little*)
Alright, I guess I will. Thanks, Doug.

DOUG exits.

THERAPIST
Our time is up for today, anyway. But I don't want to leave you with all these fears. Remember that no matter what happens in a dream, it cannot kill you. I don't know how many times I've actually died in my dreams, but I always wake up. You will too. Okay?

ELAINE
Okay. And I'll eat lots and lots of ice cream and stay up late.

THERAPIST
With a health regimen like that, you'll live to be a hundred.

THERAPIST leaves her room, but stops at the nurses' station to talk to APRIL.

THERAPIST
Who's been reading to her?

APRIL
We all do, and volunteers from town. She always has someone to read to her.

THERAPIST
You'd better supervise them more carefully. Somebody's been putting ideas in her head. About spaceships and dust and singing between the stars. It's scared her pretty bad.

APRIL
We approve everything they read. She's been reading that kind of thing for years. It's never done her any harm before. Why now?

THERAPIST
The rain, I guess. Cooped up in here, she's losing touch with reality.

DOUG passes by with a bowl of ice cream. He goes into ELAINE's room, pulls up a chair, and feeds her a spoonful.

> APRIL
>
> I know. When she's asleep, she's doing the strangest things.

> THERAPIST
>
> What kind of things?

> APRIL
>
> Oh, singing these horrible songs.

> THERAPIST
>
> What are the words?

> APRIL
>
> There aren't any words. She just sort of hums. Only the melodies are awful, not even like music. She's completely asleep. She sleeps a lot now.

> THERAPIST
>
> Listen, can we bundle her up or something? Get her outside in spite of the rain?

> APRIL
>
> It isn't just the rain. It's cold out there. And the explosion that made her like she is—it messed her up inside. She doesn't have the strength to fight off any kind of disease at all. You understand—there's a good chance that exposure to that kind of weather would kill her. And I won't take a chance on that.

> THERAPIST
>
> I'm going to be visiting her more often, then. As often as I can. She's got something going on in her head that's scaring her half to death. She thinks she's going to die.

> APRIL
>
> Bless her heart. Why would she think that?

> THERAPIST
>
> Doesn't matter. One of her imaginary friends may be getting out of hand.

APRIL
I thought you said they were harmless.

THERAPIST
They were. I'll stop by Elaine's room again before I leave here tonight. Even if she's asleep.

THERAPIST exits. DOUG gets another bite of ice cream on the spoon for ELAINE, who has continued eating during the scene. But now she shakes her head and turns her face away.

ELAINE
No more, Doug, thank you.

DOUG
Okay, no problem, kid.
(He sets down the ice cream and lowers the bed.)
You almost made me believe you like this awful stuff.

ELAINE
It was torture.

DOUG
I need to make the rounds now, but when I'm done, you up for another chess tournament?

ELAINE
I'll be here. I can beat you with my eyes closed.

DOUG exits. ELAINE closes her eyes. Light dims on ELAINE as it comes up on THERAPIST and WALLACE BAITY. Still at the Millard County Rest Home, seated in chairs in WALLACE's room.

WALLACE
So my kids don't visit much, and when they do, I remember after ten minutes that I don't much like my kids. And I have ugly grandchildren. That's the worst. All I've got left in the world is my progeny, and they look like Pomeranians.

THERAPIST
(distractedly)
How old did you say they were? Six and four? They've got some time to grow into their faces.

WALLACE

You're right, but I may not be around to see it. I almost hope I won't be. Because I don't know what the hell I'd do during all the years it'd take them to get from puppies to people. I just don't have the energy anymore. Hey, maybe I could do what you do.

THERAPIST

Mmm?

WALLACE

Get paid to pretend to listen to boring old coots while I think about my woman troubles.

THERAPIST

What? I'm listening. And I don't have woman troubles.

WALLACE

Well, I sure don't, so I guess I won't be taking your job.

THERAPIST

I'm sorry, Wallace. I was a bit preoccupied. One of my patients is having a hard time, and I'm at a loss with her right now.

WALLACE

So it *is* a woman! With troubles!

THERAPIST

Yes, I guess she is. I mean, I guess so.

WALLACE

But you can't talk about it with me.

THERAPIST

'Fraid not.

WALLACE

Is she pretty?

THERAPIST

She's my patient, I don't think about that.

WALLACE
But if she wasn't your patient, would she suddenly get pretty?

THERAPIST
I doubt I'd ever have the chance to meet her if I weren't her therapist. But. Yes. I think she would be a very pretty girl.

WALLACE
Good. If you're gonna think about a woman a lot, it helps if it's a nice-looking thought.

THERAPIST
It's a work related thought.

WALLACE
Sure, sure. You relate well to your work, most of the time.

THERAPIST
I'm sorry about that. Please continue, I'm listening.

WALLACE
Now I'm disappointed. I thought I could get you to open up and tell me about your long distance love affair with a stewardess.

THERAPIST
We should get back to *you* now, Wallace.

WALLACE
And this is what you do with youth.

Lights dim on WALLACE and THERAPIST. They exit. Lights come up on ELAINE, who is asleep. She begins her song. It is eerie. Every now and then, there are themes from the bit of Copland music she heard, but they are distorted, and most of the music is unrecognizable—not even music. Her voice is sometimes high and strange, then changes suddenly to become low and raspy.

THERAPIST enters, crosses to her room and sits in the chair by the bed. ELAINE's back arches a little with the melody, and the sounds she makes keep alternating: high and light; low and rasping.

THERAPIST reaches up and gently lifts her eyelids. ELAINE's eyes remain open, staring at the ceiling, not blinking. He closes her eyes, and they stay closed. He turns her head, and it stays turned. She does not wake up, and keeps singing

as if he has done nothing to her at all. THERAPIST leaves her room just as
DOUG passes.

> DOUG
>
> What are you doing here so late?

> THERAPIST
>
> I was checking on Elaine. She's going through a crisis of
> some kind. Do you know if the administrator is still here?
> I need to talk to him about it.

> DOUG
>
> Mr. Woodbury left already, but you could call him at home
> if it's really serious.

> THERAPIST
>
> It's really serious. Elaine could go catatonic on us at any
> moment, I think. She needs to be watched all the time.

> DOUG
>
> Wow, alright. So we need to keep her awake?

> THERAPIST
>
> As much as possible. Read to her, play with her, don't leave
> her alone. Avoid naps. Her normal hours of sleep at night
> are enough.

They exit. ELAINE's song ends. APRIL enters and raises the bed so ELAINE is
back in a seated position. ELAINE yawns sleepily, and APRIL gives her a drink
of water. Then APRIL pats ELAINE's belly and leaves the room, crossing to the
nurse's station.

Saturday afternoon. DOUG enters, sopping wet and carrying a fast food bag and
a cardboard tray of sodas.

> APRIL
>
> The hero returns.

DOUG sets the sodas down on the counter of the nurses' station. He holds up the
wet bag.

> DOUG
>
> Hope you're on a liquid diet.

APRIL

If my burger's greasy enough, the oil and water won't mix.

THERAPIST enters.

DOUG
(To THERAPIST)
Hi. Don't mention the weather.

APRIL

You're here on a Saturday?

THERAPIST

I was worried about Elaine.

APRIL

We're worried about her, too. None of us realized how much she was sleeping until we tried to stop her.

THERAPIST

How much does she sleep?

APRIL

She dozes off for two or three naps in the mornings. Even more in the afternoons.

DOUG

And she always goes to sleep at seven-thirty and sleeps at least twelve hours.

APRIL

Singing all the time. Even at night she keeps it up.

DOUG

Wish she knew some Neil Young.

THERAPIST

Thank you for your vigilance. I'm hoping it won't take long for this phase to pass.

He enters ELAINE's room.

ELAINE

I stayed awake for you.

THERAPIST
Thanks.

ELAINE
A Saturday visit. I must really be going bonkers.

THERAPIST
Actually, no. But I don't like how sleepy you are.

ELAINE
It isn't my idea.

THERAPIST
And I think it's all in your head.

ELAINE
Think what you like, Doctor.

THERAPIST
I'm not a doctor. My degree says I'm a master.

ELAINE
How deep is the water outside?

THERAPIST
Deep?

ELAINE
All this rain. Surely it's enough to keep a few dozen arks afloat. How long would it have to rain to fill up the world?

THERAPIST
The world is round. It would all drip off the bottom.

She laughs, but it ends abruptly.

ELAINE
I'm going, you know.

THERAPIST
You are?

ELAINE
I'm just the right size. She's measured me, and I'll fit

perfectly. She has just the place for me. It's a good place, where I can hear the music of the dust for myself, and learn to sing it. I'd have the directional engines.

THERAPIST
Grunty the ice pig was cute. This isn't cute, Elaine.

ELAINE
Did I ever say I thought Anansa was cute? Grunty the ice pig was real, you know. My father made him out of crushed ice for a luau. He melted before they got the pig out of the ground. I don't make my friends up.

THERAPIST
Fuchsia the flower girl?

ELAINE
My mother would pinch the blossoms off the fuchsia by our front door. We played with them like dolls in the grass.

THERAPIST
But not Anansa.

ELAINE
Anansa came into my mind when I was asleep. She found me. I didn't make her up.

THERAPIST
Don't you see, Elaine, that's how hallucinations come? They feel like reality.

ELAINE
I know all that. I've had the nurses read me psychology books. Anansa is—Anansa is other. She couldn't come out of my head. She's something else. She's real. I've heard her music. It isn't plain, like Copland. It isn't false.

THERAPIST
Elaine, when you were asleep on Wednesday, you were becoming catatonic.

ELAINE
I know.

THERAPIST
You know?

ELAINE
I felt you touch me. I felt you turn my head. I wanted to speak to you, to say goodbye. But she was singing, don't you see? And now she lets me sing along. I can feel myself travel out, like a spider along a single thread, out into the place where she is. Into the darkness. It's lonely there, and black, and cold, but I know that at the end of the thread there she'll be, a friend for me forever.

THERAPIST
You're frightening me, Elaine.

ELAINE
There aren't any trees on her starship, you know. That's how I stay here. I think of the trees and the hills and the birds and the grass and the wind, and how I'd lose all of that. She gets angry at me, and a little hurt. But it keeps me here. Except now I can hardly remember the trees at all. I try to remember, and it's like I'm trying to remember the face of my mother. I can remember her dress and her hair, but her face is gone forever. Even when I look at a picture, it's a stranger.

He strokes her forehead. At first she pulls her head away, then slides it back.

ELAINE
I'm sorry. I usually don't like people to touch me there.

THERAPIST
I won't.

ELAINE
No, go ahead. I don't mind.

He strokes her forehead again. This time she lifts her head a little to receive the touch.

ELAINE
Hold me here. Don't let me go. I want to go so badly. But I'm not meant for that. I'm just the right size, but not the right shape. Those aren't my arms. I know what my arms felt like.

THERAPIST
I'll hold you if I can. But you have to help.

ELAINE
No drugs. The drugs pull my mind away from my body. If you give me drugs, I'll die.

THERAPIST
Then what can I do?

ELAINE
Just keep me here, any way you can.

THERAPIST
It might involve Trivial Pursuit and sock puppets.

ELAINE
That's fine. I think I've played every board game ever invented. I've gotten pretty good at chess lately. I tell the nurses where to move my pieces. They hate checkmating themselves.

THERAPIST
We are all but your humble pawns, milady.

ELAINE
Everyone's trying their best to give me things to do, to look forward to. They're running out of ideas, though. I mean, how rare is it to bring someone to church meetings so they'll stay awake?

THERAPIST
I didn't know you were religious.

ELAINE
I'm not. But what else is there to do on a Sunday? They sing hymns, and I sing with them. Last Sunday there was a sermon that really got to me. The preacher talked about Christ in the sepulchre. About Him being there three days before the angel came to let Him go. I've been thinking about that, what it must have been like for Him, locked in a cave in the darkness, completely alone.

THERAPIST
Depressing.

ELAINE
Not really. It must have been exhilarating for Him, in a way.
If it was true, you know. To lie there on that stone bed, saying to Himself, "They thought I was dead, but I'm here. I'm
not dead."

THERAPIST
You make Him sound smug.

ELAINE
Sure. Why not? I wonder if I'd feel like that, if I were with
Anansa. (*pause*) I can see what you're thinking. You're
thinking, "Anansa again."

THERAPIST
Yeah. I wish you'd erase her and go back to some more
harmless friends.

ELAINE
(*Suddenly angry and fierce*)
You can believe what you like. Just leave me alone.

THERAPIST
Elaine, I'm sorry. I don't believe in Anansa, but I do believe
you can beat these nightmares. We just—

ELAINE
You heard what I said.

THERAPIST
Leave you alone.

ELAINE sets her jaw and stares straight ahead.

THERAPIST
Okay, Elaine. For today. Not for long.

*THERAPIST leaves the room as lights dim on ELAINE. He speaks to the audi-
ence downstage, as APRIL and DOUG enter to rock the nurse's station forward,
so that it becomes the couch.*

THERAPIST
The rest of that afternoon and evening I was useless. I couldn't concentrate on anything. I kept picturing Elaine with wires coming out of her shoulders and hips, with her head encased in metal and her eyes closed in sleep, piloting a starship as if it were her own body. I needed a good distraction. I called Becky. (*BECKY enters, holding a Chinese food carton and chopsticks, and sits on the couch.*) We hadn't seen each other all month. She agreed to dinner and a movie.

THERAPIST takes off his jacket, sets it on the couch, and sits. He stares ahead, watching television. BECKY keeps glancing at the show while poking her chopsticks around in a carton.

BECKY
Chinese takeout and HBO at my own apartment. Could I be a cheaper date?

THERAPIST
Sure. You could've put out before we ordered.

She feigns stabbing him in the chest with a chopstick.

THERAPIST
What? I'm trying to make you feel better.

BECKY
Then you're a terrible therapist.

THERAPIST
Don't I know it.

BECKY
Oh, honey, come on. I'm kidding! You're great at what you do. You're just a little insensitive toward my virtue.

THERAPIST
I think you're incredibly virtuous to put up with me.

BECKY
How could I resist, when your first phone call to me in a month started with, "Hi, Becky. Are you married or anything?"

THERAPIST
A lot can change in a month.

BECKY
Ha, but not with us. I'm glad you called, though. And I'm glad you're talking again. I could tell you were awake when you were chewing, but near the end of the show I thought you might have learned to sleep with your eyes open.

THERAPIST
It came in handy during the war.

BECKY
You're more upset than you're letting on. Talk to me.

THERAPIST
You've heard the gist of it. I cannot stop thinking about Elaine and her delusions about this—starwoman. I don't know how long can she hold out against the Anansa dream.

BECKY
She has the people at the rest home. You said they all love her to pieces. And she has you. She can see she still has good things.

THERAPIST
She needs trees more than she needs me.

BECKY
Besides, she can't actually *go* anywhere. With Anansa. You have time to figure out how to help her. And the rain will dry up soon. It's been almost two weeks.

THERAPIST
You're right. I need to stop brooding. I wanted your company so I could get out of this funk.

BECKY
(*suggestively*)
You wanted my—company?

She swings her legs up into his lap.

THERAPIST
Yes, I did. Don't do your Groucho eyebrows at me.

She grabs a chopstick and holds it like a cigar.

>   BECKY
>   *(In a Groucho Marx voice)*
>   I could never keep company with a man who'd choose *me*
>   for a companion.

>   THERAPIST
>   That was very, very bad.

>   BECKY
>   *(Scooching over and into his lap)*
>   I thought you liked it when I was bad.

>   THERAPIST
>   I thought the guy was supposed to say the cheesy lines.

>   BECKY
>   I'm on your lap, guy. You know what you're supposed to do.

>   THERAPIST
>   Ask what you want for Christmas?

She laughs, and kisses him. After a few moments, THERAPIST breaks off the kiss.

>   BECKY
>   What? Don't you want to?

>   THERAPIST
>   I don't know. I just—feel sad. It's grief. Like Elaine's dead,
>   and I could have saved her.

>   BECKY
>   Ah. Elaine.
>   *(She takes her legs off his lap.)*
>   But she's *not* dead. She just sleeps a lot.

>   THERAPIST
>   She said to keep her here, any way I can. But I'm a pretty
>   pathetic rescuer. Too bad this isn't a fairy tale. I could just
>   wake her up with a kiss and she'd live happily ever after.
>   Real life ain't so easy.

BECKY

Of course not. The fairy tales get it wrong.

THERAPIST

Right. No magic kisses.

BECKY

You don't wake the princess with a kiss. You wake her with
a promise.

THERAPIST

A promise. The happily ever after?

BECKY

In your arms, she'll be safe forever. If she didn't know it was
true, she'd stick with eternal slumber.

THERAPIST

Did you come up with this in graduate school?

BECKY

I've spent years getting the kiss without the promise. But I
know the difference.

THERAPIST

Becky—

BECKY

It's late. You should go home.
            (*THERAPIST stands, puts on his jacket, starts to leave*)
Call me sometime.

*THERAPIST crosses back to BECKY and kisses her one last time, then exits.
BECKY sits for a moment on the couch alone, and then lights fade and she exits.
Lights up on THERAPIST as he enters again and stands downstage left. While
THERAPIST speaks, DOUG and APRIL enter to return the "couch" to its orig-
inal position as the nurse's station. Then DOUG lays ELAINE's bed flat again
while APRIL seats herself on the downstage stool in ELAINE's room.*

THERAPIST

I didn't go back to Elaine on Sunday like I'd planned. I
spent the entire day almost going. Why was I afraid?
Unprofessional to get emotionally involved with a patient.
But then, how could I live with myself, if I let the princess

lie there unawakened because the happily ever after was so damnably much work?

At last it was Wednesday.

ELAINE begins to sing. THERAPIST enters ELAINE's room. APRIL sits on the stool, knitting.

> APRIL
> You're late.

> THERAPIST
> Rain.

> APRIL
> We hoped you'd come yesterday, but we couldn't reach you anywhere. Elaine hasn't woken up since Monday morning.

> THERAPIST
> I'd like some time alone with her, if I may.

> APRIL
> Of course. *(She leaves the room and goes to the nurse's station.)*

> THERAPIST
> Elaine.
> *(He waits for a response. Nothing but singing.)*
> Elaine.

He touches her head. Then he rocks her head back and forth. Her head stays wherever he places it.

> THERAPIST
> *(more forcefully)*
> Elaine.

He shakes her by the shoulders.

> THERAPIST
> Elaine!

APRIL can't bear to hear more; overcome with emotion, she exits the stage. THERAPIST stands by the bed, stricken.

THERAPIST
She's gone.

He crosses behind the bed to her other side. As he speaks, he eventually comes to kneel beside her.

THERAPIST
Open your eyes, Elaine. Tell me about the crazy dream you had. Laugh that you fooled me. Laugh. (*A long pause.*) Anansa, let her go. Let her come back to me. Please. I need her.

He makes his decision, and cradles ELAINE's head in one arm, stroking her cheek.

THERAPIST
If you come back, Elaine, there'll be no more rain. You'll have trees and flowers and hills and birds and the wind in your hair for as long as you like. I'll take you away from here. I'll take you to see things you've only dreamed about before. I promise you everything in this world. But you have to come back to it. Please, Elaine. (*He is speaking through tears, but as if he doesn't even realize he's crying.*) You have me. I promise you that. You have my love forever. And I promise it's stronger than any songs Anansa can sing.

ELAINE falls silent. She does not awaken, but her head rocks to the side. THERAPIST, exhausted, leans his head against the bed. He closes his eyes. But ELAINE's eyes open. She turns and notices THERAPIST. She looks down at him and smiles. Then she turns to look out the window. At that moment, APRIL returns to the nurse's station.

ELAINE
What a liar you are! It's still raining.

THERAPIST snaps his eyes open to stare at her. APRIL hears ELAINE's voice and rushes into the room.

APRIL
Elaine! You scared us to death! How do you feel?

ELAINE
I'm feeling—a lot.

APRIL
You must be.

    (*To* THERAPIST)
I don't know how you did it, but that's what you say about miracles, isn't it? I'm getting Mr. Woodbury. (*She exits.*)

        ELAINE
Hi.

        THERAPIST
Hi.

        ELAINE
So this is you.

        THERAPIST
Yes, this is what my hair looks like when I sleep on it.

        ELAINE
No more sleeping for me.

        THERAPIST
Probably not for a while.

DOUG *runs in.*

        DOUG
Elaine! April just told me. I thought we'd never get you back.

        ELAINE
Well, I'm here for good.

        DOUG
Are you hungry? I'll bring you any food from anywhere in the world.

        ELAINE
I don't know yet. Can you ask me later?

        DOUG
I can and I will. *(He turns to* THERAPIST*)* Are you going to publish?

        THERAPIST
No. It's too personal.

DOUG
(*Shaking THERAPIST's hand*)
You don't see something like this every day. Good going, man.

DOUG exits.

ELAINE
What was that?

THERAPIST
Just a short meeting of the Nobel Prize committee.

ELAINE
They want to reward you for bringing me here?

THERAPIST
Oh, no. They had been planning to give me the award for contacting a genuine alien. Instead, I blew it and brought you back. They're quite upset.

ELAINE
(*flustered*)
But what will they do to you?

THERAPIST
Probably boil me in oil. Though, maybe they've found a way to boil me in solar energy. It's cheaper.

ELAINE
This isn't the way she said it was—she said it was—

THERAPIST
She said? Who said?

ELAINE falls silent.

THERAPIST
What's wrong? You're upset.

ELAINE
I should have known.

THERAPIST
Known what?

She shakes her head and turns away from him.

THERAPIST
Anansa didn't go away, is that it?

ELAINE
Yes. That's it.

THERAPIST
So you're not completely cured yet. I guess that would have been too much of a miracle. We've just made progress, that's all. Brought you back from catalepsy. We'll free you of Anansa eventually. Don't worry, I'm a grown-up. I can cope with a little disappointment. Besides, you're awake, you're back, that's all that matters. So don't go feeling guilty about it.

ELAINE
Guilty?
(Her chuckle is ironic and bitter.)
Guilty.

THERAPIST
You tried to do the right thing.

ELAINE
Did I? Did I really? I meant to stay with her. I wanted her with me, she was so alive, and when she finally joined herself to the ship, she sang and danced and swung her arms, and I said, "This is what I've needed. This is what I've craved all my centuries lost in the songs." But then I heard *you*.

The realization hits him, and THERAPIST puts his hand to ELAINE's forehead. She does not react.

THERAPIST
Anansa.

ELAINE
I heard *you*, crying out to her. Do you think I made up my mind quickly? She heard you, but she wouldn't come. She wouldn't trade her new arms and legs for anything. They were so new. But I'd had them long enough. What I'd never had was—you.

THERAPIST
Where is she?

ELAINE
Out there. She sings better than I ever did. And I'm here. Only I made a bad bargain, didn't I? Because I didn't fool you. You won't want me, now. It's Elaine you want, and she's gone. I left her alone out there. She won't mind, not for a long time. But then—then she will. Then she'll know I cheated her.

THERAPIST
How did you cheat her?

ELAINE
It never changes. In a while you learn all the songs, and they never change. Nothing moves. You go on forever until all the stars fail, and yet nothing ever moves.

THERAPIST
Oh, God.
(*He reaches a trembling hand to his hair.*)

ELAINE
You hate me.

He shakes his head but can't quite speak.

ELAINE
I'd undo it if I could. But I can't. She's gone, and I'm here. I came because of you. I came to see the trees and the grass and the birds and your smile. The happily ever after. That was what she had lived for, you know, all she lived for. Please smile at me.

The sound of the rain stops at last. THERAPIST lifts his head and looks out the window.

THERAPIST
Let's go outside.

ELAINE
It stopped raining.

THERAPIST
(*He smiles ruefully.*)
A bit late, isn't it?

ELAINE
You can call me Elaine. You won't tell, will you?

THERAPIST
No, I won't tell.

ELAINE looks at him a moment, then shakes her head.

ELAINE
I don't mind. Whatever you want to believe: Elaine or Anansa. Maybe it's better if you still look for Elaine. Maybe it's better if you let me fool you after all.
(*She smiles at him.*)
I'm Elaine. I'm Elaine, pretending to be Anansa. You love me. That's what I came for. Take me outside. You made it stop raining for me. You did everything you promised, and I'm home again, and I promise I'll never leave you.

ELAINE freezes. THERAPIST steps away, out of the scene. As he speaks, he ends up downstage center.

THERAPIST
She hasn't left me. I come to see her every Wednesday as part of my work, and every Saturday and Sunday as the best part of my life. None of the nurses know that she is still unwell—to them she's Elaine, happier than ever, pathetically delighted at every sight and sound and smell and taste and every texture that they touch against her cheek. Only *I* know that she believes she is not Elaine. Only *I* know that I have made no progress at all since then, that in moments of terrible honesty I call her Anansa, and she sadly answers me.

After a few weeks, I realized that she had the best of all possible worlds, for her. She could tell herself that the real Elaine was off in space somewhere, dancing and singing, with arms and legs at last, while the poor girl who was confined to the limbless body was really an alien who was very, very happy to have even that.

And as for me, I kept my commitment to her, and I'm happier for it. I'm still human—I still take another woman to my bed from time to time. But Anansa doesn't mind. She even suggested it. So there aren't really any discontentments in my life.

(*Pause*)

Except that I'm not God. I would like to be God. I would make some changes.

When I go to the Millard County Rest Home, I never enter the building first.

THERAPIST crosses upstage as DOUG and APRIL enter. As THERAPIST continues to speak, DOUG and APRIL pick up ELAINE so that she ends up seated in their arms. They carry her downstage center, and set her on her feet, but stay at either side of her with their hands behind her back for support. ELAINE faces front, as if watching THERAPIST from across the yard.

THERAPIST

I walk around the outside and look across the lawn by the trees. The wheelchair is always there. I never call out. In a few moments she always sees me, and they wheel her around and push the chair across the lawn. She comes as she has come hundreds of times before. She plunges toward me, and I concentrate on watching her, so that my mind won't see my Elaine surrounded by blackness, plunging through space, with her new arms and legs that she loves better than me. Instead I watch the smile on her face.

(*ELAINE grins in recognition*)

She is happy to see me, so delighted with the world outside that her body cannot contain her. And then I *am* God for a moment.

(*As THERAPIST speaks, DOUG and APRIL each remove one of ELAINE's gloves.*)

I give her a left hand and then a right hand, and she waves to me.

(*ELAINE waves, then bends over to pull down her stockings.*)

I put a pair of sturdy legs on her, and I see her running toward me.

ELAINE

(*Bouncing and beckoning to him excitedly*)

Hurry up, you're using the whole Wednesday just getting over here!

THERAPIST
And then, one by one, I take them all away.

ELAINE stands still, drops her arms to her sides.

The lights go down.

THE END

AFTERWORD

by Emily Janice Card

I first read "A Sepulchre of Songs" when I was fifteen years old. Immediately it became for me one of those stories you feel you always knew had to exist, and yet are in awe that someone actually wrote it down so that you could find it when you needed it.

At a time when I felt trapped in an awkward, ugly adolescent body, and made grand pronouncements from the bathroom that no one would ever understand or love me so don't make me go to school, I discovered this limbless girl, limited more than I would ever be, and I related completely.

Granted, since my father wrote it, I had to swallow some of my melodramatic pride and admit that my parents might actually understand my hard hard life. One of many lessons I learned because of this story.

I had always thought "Sepulchre" would make a wonderful movie, but the digital effects required to make the actress's arms and legs disappear would cost much more than anyone would be likely to spend on a small, talky and only slightly science fictional film.

Then, after participating in good plays where we had almost no set and used large wooden blocks to represent most furniture, flora, and geology, I started to think of how "Sepulchre" could work on stage, since theatrical effects are not limited by realism the way movies are.

The idea came to have Elaine put on white gloves and stockings in front of the audience to "disappear" her own arms and legs. I told my dad. He said, "Great! So write it."

Another lesson: Do not write as if every tap on the computer keyboard will make blood gush from your fingertips.

First, because you will never finish anything.

And second, because you will fate yourself to only complete projects when you really do mutilate your body in some way. I could not have adapted this play without that handy tonsillectomy. (I'm picking at a scab right now so I can finish this afterword today.)

Dad said that the best way to start writing plays is to adapt existing material. And "Sepulchre" was the best existing material for me, novice playwright, to tackle, since at its core it is a dialogue between Elaine and her therapist. The biggest chunk of the play was already there, and all I had to do was turn the prose surrounding those conversations into…more conversations.

The hardest creative decision for me was just allowing the therapist to narrate, because so often narration is used to get around lazy writing. But much of the story's power came from the interior journey of the therapist, and for the audience to understand the choice he ultimately makes, we need him to tell us what's going on in his head.

An added bonus was that he could control the flow of time through his monologues, so that the play didn't seem like one long day of him just popping in and out of Elaine's room.

And the great thing, after all these little choices in the writing, was to see what this amazing cast did with the roles they had. They took these characters and these "extra conversations" and transformed them into moments with way more life history than the play hinted at.

Crotchety Wallace Baity with a Polish accent and an all-knowing twinkle in his eye? Absolutely, thanks to Stefan Rudnicki.

Eric Artell brought more than the requisite humor to Doug; the joking came from compassion, and he always appeared smart and good at the job.

April the head nurse was supposed to be middle-aged and matronly, yet that hot young thing Kelly Lohman had all the warmth and wisdom of a mature woman, while anchoring the play in the reality of a rest home better than even the most elaborate set could have done.

When I first wrote the scene with Becky, I had imagined her becoming distant and self-protective as she explained to the therapist why the fairy tales are wrong; instead, Lara Schwartzberg infused her words with love and longing, and made Becky the tragic heroine of her own story.

And I hadn't known it was possible to turn narration and listening into something so mesmerizingly, energetically intimate until I watched Kirby Heyborne do it every night.

As for me, playing Elaine was the toughest acting I've done so far, and I knew going into it that I probably wasn't ready. But I also knew, with my father as director and with this cast, there would never be a more ideal and supportive setting for me to try to get there.

Lying on that bed for a whole show was strange on the butt *and* acting muscles, and having only my face, head, neck, shoulders and voice as performing tools was a big challenge.

I learned that because I only had those things to work with, it was more effective to use them sparingly, but with great intent. For instance, a suggestion by my dad to take most of the breath out of my voice when I became Anansa helped me find her entire character.

The weird singing of the starship was harder to create and sustain, because I really didn't want Elaine to pause or breathe in any noticeable way that might seem like she was aware of or reacting to anything around her. Luckily, I stole Jack Black's technique of "inward singing" from a Tenacious D album and figured out how to breathe in while still making sound. Once I got enough practice, I relished being so incredibly obnoxious.

Of course, all the rehearsal in the world didn't prepare me for the shock of seeing my own legs disappear, once I had them underneath a blanket and in the hidey-hole our set designer, Cristian Bell, thought up and built into the bed. At our first rehearsal with the bed, I forgot my first line because I glanced down at the empty space beyond my knees and freaked out. That's when you know a show is working.

And now I come back to that same awe, and gratitude, for an experience that comes along just when you need it. To play a part that meant so much to me, at the last possible moment in my life when I could pass as a teenager, and to have my dad give me his story to work on as my own, and then also direct me in the role . . . dream, dream, all a dream.

Three Stories

CLAP HANDS AND SING

by Orson Scott Card

On the screen the crippled man screamed at the lady, insisting that she must not run away. He waved a certificate. "I'm a registered rapist, damnit!" he cried. "Don't run so fast! You have to make allowances for the handi-capped!" He ran after her with an odd, left-heavy lope. His enormous pros-thetic phallus swung crazily, like a clumsy propeller that couldn't quite get started. The audience laughed madly. Must be a funny, funny scene!

Old Charlie sat slumped in his chair, feeling as casual and permanent as glacial debris. *I am here only by accident, but I'll never move.* He did not switch off the television set. The audience roared again with laughter. Canned or live? After more than eight decades of watching television, Charlie couldn't tell anymore. Not that the canned laughter had got any more real: It was the real laughter that had gone tinny, premeditated. As if the laughs were timed to come *now*, no matter what, and the poor actors could strain to get off their gags in time, but always they were just *this* much early, *that* much late.

"It's late," the television said, and Charlie started awake, vaguely sur-prised to see that the program had changed: Now it was a demonstration of a convenient electric breast pump to store up natural mother's milk for those times when you just can't be with baby. "It's late."

"Hello, Jock," Charlie said.

"Don't sleep in front of the television again, Charlie."

"Leave me alone, swine," Charlie said. And then: "Okay, turn it off."

He hadn't finished giving the order when the television flickered and went white, then settled down into its perpetual springtime scene that meant *off*. But in the flicker Charlie thought he saw—who? Name? From the distant past. A girl. Before the name came to him, there came another memory: a small hand resting lightly on his knee as they sat together, as light as a long-legged fly upon a stream. In his memory he did not turn to look at her; he was talking to others. But he knew just where she would be if he turned to look. Small, with mousy hair, and yet a face that was always the child Juliet. But that was not her name. Not Juliet, though she was Juliet's age in that memory. *I am Charlie,* he thought. *She is—Rachel.*

Rachel Carpenter. In the flicker on the screen hers was the face the random light had brought him, and so he remembered Rachel as he pulled his ancient body from the chair; thought of Rachel as he peeled the clothing from his frail skeleton, delicately, lest some rough motion strip away the wrinkled skin like cellophane.

And Jock, who of course did not switch himself off with the television, recited:

"An aged man is a paltry thing, a tattered coat upon a stick."

"Shut up," Charlie ordered.

"Unless Soul clap its hands."

"I said shut up!"

"And sing, and louder sing, for every tatter in its mortal dress."

"Are you finished?" Charlie asked. He knew Jock was finished. After all, Charlie had programmed him to recite—*it* to recite—just that fragment every night when his shorts hit the floor.

He stood naked in the middle of the room and thought of Rachel, whom he had not thought of in years. It was a trick of being old, that the room he was in now so easily vanished, and in its place a memory could take hold. *I've made my fortune from time machines,* he thought, *and now I discover that every aged person is his own time machine.* For now he stood naked. No, that was a trick of memory; memory had these damnable tricks. He was not naked. He only felt naked, as Rachel sat in the car beside him. Her voice—he had almost forgotten her voice—was soft. Even when she shouted, it got more whispery, so that if she shouted, it would have all the wind of the world in it and he wouldn't hear it at all, would only feel it cold on his naked skin. That was the voice she was using now, saying yes. I loved you when I was twelve, and when I was thirteen, and when I was fourteen, but when you got back from playing God in Sao Paulo, you didn't call me. All those letters, and then for three months you didn't call me and I knew that you thought I was just a child and I fell in love with—Name? Name gone. Fell in love with a *boy,* and ever since then you've been treating me like. Like. No, she'd never say *shit,* not in that voice. And take some of the anger out, that's right. Here are the words … here they come: You could have had me, Charlie, but now all you can do is try to make me miserable. It's too late, the time's gone by, the time's over, so stop criticizing me. Leave me *alone.*

First to last, all in a capsule. The words are nothing, Charlie realized. A dozen women, not least his dear departed wife, had said exactly the same words to him since, and it had sounded just as maudlin, just as unpleasantly uninteresting every time. The difference was that when the others said it, Charlie felt himself insulated with a thousand layers of unconcern. But when

Rachel said it to his memory, he stood naked in the middle of his room, a cold wind drying the parchment of his ancient skin.

"What's wrong?" asked Jock.

Oh, yes, dear computer, a change in the routine of the habitbound old man, and you suspect what, a heart attack? Incipient death? Extreme disorientation?

"A name," Charlie said. "Rachel Carpenter."

"Living or dead?"

Charlie winced again, as he winced every time Jock asked that question; yet it was an important one, and far too often the answer these days was Dead. "I don't know."

"Living and dead, I have two thousand four hundred eighty in the company archives alone."

"She was twelve when I was—twenty. Yes, twenty. And she lived then in Provo, Utah. Her father was a pianist. Maybe she became an actress when she grew up. She wanted to."

"Rachel Carpenter. Born 1959. Provo, Utah. Attended—"

"Don't show off, Jock. Was she ever married?"

"Thrice."

"And don't imitate my mannerisms. Is she still alive?"

"Died ten years ago."

Of course. Dead, of course. He tried to imagine her—where? "Where did she die?"

"Not pleasant."

"Tell me anyway. I'm feeling suicidal tonight."

"In a home for the mentally incapable."

It was not shocking; people often outlived their minds these days. But sad. For she had always been bright. Strange perhaps, but her thoughts always led to something worth the sometimes-convoluted path. He smiled even before he remembered what he was smiling at. Yes. Seeing through your knees. She had been playing Helen Keller in *The Miracle Worker*, and she told him how she had finally come to understand blindness. "It isn't seeing the red insides of your eyelids, I knew that. I knew it isn't even seeing black. It's like trying to see where you never had eyes at all. Seeing through your knees. No matter how hard you try, there just isn't any *vision* there." And she had liked him because he hadn't laughed. "I told my brother, and he laughed," she said. But Charlie had not laughed.

Charlie's affection for her had begun then, with a twelve-year-old girl who could never stay on the normal, intelligible track, but rather had to stumble her own way through a confusing underbrush that was thick and bright with flowers. "I think God stopped paying attention long ago," she said. "Any more than Michelangelo would want to watch them whitewash the Sistine Chapel."

And he knew that he would do it even before he knew what it was that he would do. She had ended in an institution, and he, with the best medical care that money could buy, stood naked in his room and remembered when passion still lurked behind the lattices of chastity and was more likely to lead to poems than to coitus.

You overtold story, he said to the wizened man who despised him from the mirror. You are only tempted because you're bored. Making excuses because you're cruel. Lustful because your dim old dong is long past the exercise.

And he heard the old bastard answer silently, You *will* do it, because you can. Of all the people in the world, *you* can.

And he thought he saw Rachel look back at him, bright with finding herself beautiful at fourteen, laughing at the vast joke of knowing she was admired by the very man whom she, too, wanted. Laugh all you like, Charlie said to the vision of her. I was too kind to you then. I'm afraid I'll undo my youthful goodness now.

"I'm going back," he said aloud. "Find me a day."

"For what purpose?" Jock asked.

"My business."

"I have to know your purpose, or how can I find you a day?"

And so he had to name it. "I'm going to have her if I can."

Suddenly a small alarm sounded, and Jock's voice was replaced by another. "Warning. Illegal use of THIEF for possible present-altering manipulation of the past."

Charlie smiled. "Investigation has found that the alteration is acceptable. Clear." And the program release: "Byzantium."

"You're a son of a bitch," said Jock.

"Find me a day. A day when the damage will be least—when I can…"

"Twenty-eight October 1973."

That was after he got home from Sao Paulo, the contracts signed and read, already a capitalist before he was twenty-three. That was during the time when he had been afraid to call her, because she was only fourteen, for God's sake.

"What will it do to her, Jock?"

"How should I know?" Jock answered. "And what difference would it make to you?"

He looked in the mirror again. "A difference."

I won't do it, he told himself as he went to the THIEF that was his most ostentatious sign of wealth, a private THIEF in his own rooms. I won't do it, he decided again as he set the machine to wake him in twelve hours, whether he wished to return or not. Then he climbed into the couch and pulled the shroud over his head, despairing that even this, even doing it to *her*, was not beneath him. There was a time when he had automatically held back from doing a thing because he knew that it was wrong. *Oh, for that time!* he thought, but knew as he thought it that he was lying to himself. He had long since given up on right and wrong and settled for the much simpler standards of effective and ineffective, beneficial and detrimental.

He had gone in a THIEF before, had taken some of the standard trips into the past. Gone into the mind of an audience member of the first performance of Handel's *Messiah* and listened. The poor soul whose ears he used wouldn't remember a bit of it afterward. So the future would not be changed. That was safe, to sit in a hall and listen. He had been in the mind of a farmer resting under a tree on a country lane as Wordsworth walked by and had hailed the poet and asked his name, and Wordsworth had smiled and been distant and cold, delighting in the countryside more than in those whose tillage made it beautiful. But those were legal trips—Charlie had done nothing that could alter the course of history.

This time, though. This time he would change Rachel's life. Not his own, of course. That would be impossible. But Rachel would not be blocked from remembering what happened. She would remember, and it would turn her from the path she was meant to take. Perhaps only a little. Perhaps not importantly. Perhaps just enough for her to dislike him a little sooner, or a little more. But too much to be legal, if he were caught.

He would not be caught. Not Charlie. Not the man who owned THIEF and therefore could have owned the world. It was all too bound up in secrecy. Too many agents had used his machines to attend the enemy's most private conferences. Too often the Attorney General had listened to the most perfect of wiretaps. Too often politicians who were willing to be in Charlie's debt had been given permission to lead their opponents into blunders that cost them votes. All far beyond what the law allowed; who would dare complain now if Charlie also bent the law to his own purpose?

No one but Charlie. *I can't do this to Rachel,* he thought. And then the THIEF carried him back and put him into his own mind, in his own body, on 28 October 1973, at ten o'clock, just as he was going to bed, weary because he had been wakened that morning by a six A.M. call from Brazil.

As always, there was the moment of resistance, and then peace as his self of that time slipped into unconsciousness. Old Charlie took over and saw, not the past, but the now.

◆ ◆ ◆

A moment before, he was standing before a mirror, looking at his withered, hanging face; now he realizes that this gazing into a mirror before going to bed is a lifelong habit. *I am Narcissus,* he tells himself, *an unbeautiful idolator at my own shrine.* But now he is not unbeautiful. At twenty-two, his body still has the depth of young skin. His belly is soft, for he is not athletic, but still there is a litheness to him that he will never have again. And now the vaguely remembered needs that had impelled him to this find a physical basis; what had been a dim memory has him on fire.

He will not be sleeping tonight, not soon. He dresses again, finding with surprise the quaint print shirts that once had been in style. The wide-cuffed pants. The shoes with inch-and-a-half heels. *Good God, I wore that!* he thinks, and then wears it. No questions from his family; he goes quietly downstairs and out to his car. The garage reeks of gasoline. It is a smell as nostalgic as lilacs and candlewax.

He still knows the way to Rachel's house, though he is surprised at the buildings that have not yet been built, which roads have not yet been paved, which intersections still don't have lights he knows they'll have soon, should surely have already. He looks at his wristwatch; it must be a habit of the body he is in, for he hasn't worn a wristwatch in decades. The arm is tanned from Brazilian beaches, and it has no age spots, no purple veins drawing roadmaps under the skin. The time is ten-thirty. *She'll doubtless be in bed.*

He almost stops himself. Few things are left in his private catalog of sin, but surely this is one. He looks into himself and tries to find the will to resist his own desire solely because its fulfillment will hurt another person. He is out of practice—so far out of practice that he keeps losing track of the reason for resisting.

The lights are on, and her mother—Mrs. Carpenter, dowdy and delightful, scatterbrained in the most attractive way—her mother opens the door suspiciously until she recognizes him. "Charlie," she cries out.

"Is Rachel up?"

"Give me a minute and she will be!"

And he waits, his stomach trembling with anticipation. *I am not a virgin,* he reminds himself, *but this body does not know that.* This body is alert, for it has not yet formed the habits of meaningless passion that Charlie knows far too well. At last she comes down the stairs. He hears her running on the hollow wooden steps, then stopping, coming slowly, denying the hurry. She turns the corner, looks at him.

She is in her bathrobe, a faded thing that he does not remember ever having seen her wear. Her hair is tousled, and her eyes show that she had been asleep.

"I didn't mean to wake you."

"I wasn't really asleep. The first ten minutes don't count anyway."

He smiles. Tears come to his eyes. Yes, he says silently. This is Rachel, yes. The narrow face; the skin so translucent that he can see into it like jade; the slender arms that gesture shyly, with accidental grace.

"I couldn't wait to see you."

"You've been home three days. I thought you'd phone."

He smiles. In fact he will not phone her for months. But he says, "I hate the telephone. I want to talk to you. Can you come out for a drive?"

"I have to ask my mother."

"She'll say yes."

She does say yes. She jokes and says that she trusts Charlie. And the Charlie she knows was trustworthy. *But not me,* Charlie thinks. You are putting your diamonds into the hands of a thief.

"Is it cold?" Rachel asks.

"Not in the car." And so she doesn't take a coat. It's all right. The night breeze isn't bad.

As soon as the door closes behind them, Charlie begins. He puts his arm around her waist. She does not pull away or take it with indifference. He has never done this before, because she's only fourteen, just a child, but she leans against him as they walk, as if she had done this a hundred times before. As always, she takes him by surprise.

"I've missed you," he says.

She smiles, and there are tears in her eyes. "I've missed you, too," she says.

They talk of nothing. It's just as well. Charlie does not remember much about the trip to Brazil, does not remember anything of what he's done in the three days since getting back. No problem, for she seems to want to talk only of tonight. They drive to the Castle, and he tells her its history. He feels an irony about it as he explains. She, after all, is the reason he knows the history. A few years from now she will be part of a theater company that revives the Castle as a public amphitheater. But now it is falling into ruin, a monument to the old WPA, a great castle with turrets and benches made of native stone. It is on the property of the state mental hospital, and so hardly anyone knows it's there. They are alone as they leave the car and walk up the crumbling steps to the flagstone stage.

She is entranced. She stands in the middle of the stage, facing the benches. He watches as she raises her hand, speech waiting at the verge of her lips. He remembers something. Yes, that is the gesture she made when she bade her nurse farewell in *Romeo and Juliet*. No, not *made*. Will make, rather. The gesture must already be in her, waiting for this stage to draw it out.

She turns to him and smiles because the place is strange and odd and does not belong in Provo, but it does belong to her. She should have been born in the Renaissance, Charlie says softly. She hears him. He must have spoken aloud. "You belong in an age when music was clean and soft and there was no makeup. No one would rival you then."

She only smiles at the conceit. "I missed you," she says.

He touches her cheek. She does not shy away. Her cheek pressed into his hand, and he knows that she understands why he brought her here and what he means to do.

Her breasts are perfect but small, her buttocks are boyish and slender, and the only hair on her body is that which tumbles onto her shoulders, that which he must brush out of her face to kiss her again. "I love you," she whispers. "All my life I love you."

And it is exactly as he would have had it in a dream, except that the flesh is tangible, the ecstasy is real, and the breeze turns colder as she shyly dresses again. They say nothing more as he takes her home. Her mother has fallen asleep on the living room couch, a jumble of the *Daily Herald* piled around her feet. Only then does he remember that for her there will be a tomorrow, and on that tomorrow Charlie did not call. For three months Charlie will not call, and she'll hate him.

He tries to soften it. He tries by saying, "Some things can happen only once." It is the sort of thing he might then have said. But she only puts her finger on his lips and says, "I'll never forget." Then she turns and walks toward her mother, to waken her. She turns and motions for Charlie to leave, then smiles again and waves. He waves back and goes out of the door and drives home. He lies awake in this bed that feels like childhood to him, and he wishes it could have gone on forever like this. *It should have gone on like this,* he thinks. *She is no child. She* was *no child,* he should have thought for THIEF was already transporting him home.

♦ ♦ ♦

"What's wrong, Charlie?" Jock asked.

Charlie awoke. It had been hours since THIEF brought him back. It was the middle of the night, and Charlie realized that he had been crying in his sleep. "Nothing," he said.

"You're crying, Charlie. I've never seen you cry before."

"Go plug into a million volts, Jock. I had a dream."

"What dream?"

"I destroyed her."

"No, you didn't."

"It was a goddamned selfish thing to do."

"You'd do it again. But it didn't hurt her."

"She was only fourteen."

"No, she wasn't."

"I'm tired. I was asleep. Leave me alone."

"Charlie, remorse isn't your style."

Charlie pulled the blanket over his head, feeling petulant and wondering whether this childish act was another proof that he was retreating into senility after all.

"Charlie, let me tell you a bedtime story."

"I'll erase you."

"Once upon a time, ten years ago, an old woman named Rachel Carpenter petitioned for a day in her past. And it was a day *with* someone, and it was a day with *you.* So the routine circuits called me, as they always do when your name comes up, and I found her a day. She only wanted to visit, you see, only wanted to relive a good day. I was surprised, Charlie. I didn't know you ever had good days."

This program had been with Jock too long. It knew too well how to get under his skin.

"And in fact there were no days as good as she thought," Jock continued. "Only anticipation and disappointment. That's all you ever gave anybody, Charlie. Anticipation and disappointment."

"I can count on you."

"This woman was in a home for the mentally incapable. And so I gave her a day. Only instead of a day of disappointment, or promises she knew would never be fulfilled, I gave her a day of answers. I gave her a night of answers, Charlie."

"You couldn't know that I'd have you do this. You couldn't have known it ten years ago."

"That's all right, Charlie. Play along with me. You're dreaming anyway, aren't you?"

"And don't wake me up."

"So an old woman went back into a young girl's body on twenty-eight October 1973, and the young girl never knew what had happened; so it didn't change her life, don't you see?"

"It's a lie."

"No, it isn't. I can't lie, Charlie. You programmed me not to lie. Do you think I would have let you go back and *harm* her?"

"She was the same. She was as I remembered her."

"Her body was."

"She hadn't changed. She wasn't an old woman, Jock. She was a girl. She was a girl, Jock."

And Charlie thought of an old woman dying in an institution, surrounded by yellow walls and pale gray sheets and curtains. He imagined young Rachel inside that withered form, imprisoned in a body that would not move, trapped in a mind that could never again take her along her bright, mysterious trails.

"I flashed her picture on the television," Jack said.

And yet, Charlie thought, *how is it less bearable than that beautiful boy who wanted so badly to do the right thing that he did it all wrong, lost his chance, and now is caught in the sum of all his wrong turns? I got on the road they all wanted to take, and I reached the top, but it wasn't where it should have gone. I'm still that boy. I did not have to lie when I went home to her.*

"I know you pretty well, Charlie," Jock said. "I knew that you'd be enough of a bastard to go back. And enough of a human being to do it right when you got there. She came back happy, Charlie. She came back satisfied."

His night with a beloved child was a lie then; it wasn't young Rachel any more than it was young Charlie. He looked for anger inside himself but couldn't find it. For a dead woman had given him a gift, and taken the one he offered, and it still tasted sweet.

"Time for sleep, Charlie. Go to sleep again. I just wanted you to know that there's no reason to feel any remorse for it. No reason to feel anything bad at all."

Charlie pulled the covers tight around his neck, unaware that he had begun that habit years ago, when the strange shadowy shapes hid in his closet and only the blanket could keep him safe. Pulled the covers high and tight, and closed his eyes, and felt her hand stroke him, felt her breast and hip and thigh, and heard her voice as breath against his chest.

"O chestnut tree," Jock said, as he had been taught to say, "…great rooted blossomer,

"Are you the leaf, the blossom, or the bole?

"O body swayed to music, O brightening glance,

"How can we know the dancer from the dance?"

The audience applauded in his mind while he slipped into sleep, and he thought it remarkable that they sounded genuine. He pictured them smiling and nodding at the show. Smiling at the girl with her hand raised so; nodding at the man who paused forever, then came on stage.

AFTERWORD TO "CLAP HANDS"

by Orson Scott Card

I don't like autobiographical fiction. It smacks of lack of imagination on the part of the author.

I especially don't like self-serving autobiographical fiction. You know, the endless literary novels about "artistic" heroes that nobody understands, who are really more intelligent and sensitive than any of the clods around them, and who always have nubile young women begging to sleep with them.

Of course, in a sense *all* fiction is autobiographical, since the only human being that any writer has ever actually lived inside of is himself. And therefore all the characters he creates are going to reflect his experiences, attitudes, and interpretations.

Somewhere between the memoire, the self-serving fantasy, and the inchoate self-confessions that are present in all fiction, there is a legitimate exploitation of one's own past in order to form the root of a story that will be more universal.

I tried for this in my novel *Lost Boys*, in which the family's experiences in Steubenville are absolutely based on our first few years in Greensboro, North Carolina. The danger, of course, is that readers who don't know that will say things like the letter I got from a Mormon who didn't like the way the Church was portrayed in that novel. "Well, if you were going to have a Mormon hero, at least you could have made him a *good* Mormon." I decided that was not the moment to mention that Step Fletcher was based on me.

"Clap Hands and Sing" is nowhere near as autobiographical as *Lost Boys*. But it did have its beginning in a situation drawn from my life.

Prior to my mission to Brazil, I had a good friendship with a young girl and several other members of her family. But she was young—thirteen when I left for my mission, fifteen when I returned, compared to my age of twenty and twenty-two, respectively. She was remarkably talented and a delightful human being whom I adored. But given her age, I didn't even consider her as a possible partner in romance. Instead, when I got home from my mission and started a theatre company, I cast her as Juliet—opposite her boyfriend at the time as Romeo.

Only later did I learn that for a time she had harbored some romantic inclinations toward me while I was on my mission (women have always found me far more attractive when there were thousands of miles between us) and was disappointed that I didn't call her right away when I returned.

The odd thing was that I specifically remembered wanting to call her, and not doing so because she was fifteen and what would her parents think—that I was trying to put the moves on their *child* when I was obviously too old for her? I decided to bide my time and see if anything developed later. But…later was too late. She had moved on. The opportunity—which I hadn't even known about—was lost.

This is hardly a tragedy for either of us—we both found true love with someone else. But after the conversation with her in which I learned about those past feelings, I—ever the sci-fi writer—wondered what it might be like if such a relationship between two characters *had* been "the love of their lives" and in old age one of them decided to go back in time and relive the moment…and change it.

So it is only the root of the situation that came from my life—the idea of missed opportunity and some of the details of their ages. I'd like to think that I'm a much nicer old guy than Charlie, and I'm definitely not rich and powerful like him. Plus, there's no such thing as time travel.

LIFELOOP

by Orson Scott Card

Arran lay on her bed, weeping. The sound of the door slamming still rang through her flat. Finally she rolled over, looked at the ceiling, wiped tears away delicately with her fingers, and then said, "What the hell."

Dramatic pause. And then, at least (at long last) a loud buzzer sounded. "All clear, Arran," said the voice from the concealed speaker, and Arran groaned, swung around to sit on the bed, unstrapped the loop recorder from her naked leg, and threw it tiredly against the wall. It smashed.

"Do you have any idea how much that equipment *costs?*" Truiff asked, reproachfully.

"I pay you to know," Arran said, putting on a robe. Truiff found the tie and handed it to her. As Arran threaded it through the loops, Truiff exulted. "The best ever. A hundred billion Arran Handully fans are aching to pay their seven chops to get in to watch. And you gave it to them."

"Seventeen days," Arran said, glaring at the other woman.

"Seventeen stinking days. And three of them with that bastard Courtney."

"He's *paid* to be a bastard. It's his persona."

"He's pretty damned convincing. If you get me even three minutes with him, next time, I'll sack you."

Arran strode out of her flat, barefoot and clad only in the robe. Truiff followed, her high-heeled shoes making a clicking rhythm that, to Arran anyway, always seemed to be saying, "Money, money, money." Except when it was saying, "Screw your mother, screw your mother." Good manager. Billions in the bank.

"Arran," Truiff said. "I know you're very tired."

"Ha," Arran said.

"But while you were recording I had time to do a little business—"

"While I was recording you had time to manufacture a planet!" Arran snarled. "Seventeen days! I'm an actress, I'm not going for the guiness. I'm the highest paid actress in history, I think you said in your latest press release. So why do I work my tail off for seventeen days when I'm only awake for twenty-one? Four lousy days of peace, and then the marathon."

"A little business," Truiff went on, unperturbed. "A little business that will let you retire."

"Retire?" And without thinking, Arran slowed down her pace.

"Retire. Imagine – awake for three weeks, and only guest appearances in other poor slobs' loops. Getting paid for having fun."

"Nights to myself?"

"We'll turn off the recorder."

Arran scowled. Truiff amended: "You can even take the thing off!"

"And what do I have to do to earn so much? Have an affair with a gorilla?"

"It's been done," Truiff said, "and it's beneath you. No, this time we give them total reality. Total!"

"What do we give them now? Sure, you want me to crap in a glass toilet!"

"I've made arrangements," Truiff said, "to have a loop recorder in the Sleeproom."

Arran Handully gasped and stared at her manager. "In the Sleeproom! Is nothing sacred!" And then Arran laughed. "You must have spent a fortune! An absolute fortune!"

"Actually, only one bribe was necessary."

"Who'd you bribe, Mother?"

"Very close. Better, in fact, since Mother hasn't got the power to pick her nose without the consent of the Cabinet. It's Farl Baak."

"Baak! And here I thought he was a decent man."

"It wasn't a bribe . At least, not for money."

Arran squinted at Truiff. "Truiff," she said, "I told you that I was willing to act out twenty-four-hour-a-day love affairs. But I chose my own lovers off-camera."

"You'll be able to retire."

"I'm not a whore!"

"And he said he wouldn't even sleep with you, if you didn't want. He just asked for twenty-four hours with you two wakings from now. To talk. To become friends."

Arran leaned against the wall of the corridor. "It'll really make that much money?"

"You forget, Arran. All your fans are in love with you. But no one has ever done what you're going to do. From a half hour before waking to a half hour after you've been put to sleep."

"Before waking and after the somec," Arran smiled. "There's nobody in the Empire who's seen that, except the Sleeproom attendants."

"And we can advertise utter reality. No illusion: you'll see *everything* that happens to Arran Handully for three weeks of waking!"

Arran thoughtfully considered for moment. "It'll be hell," she said.

"You can retire afterward," Truiff reminded her.

"All right," Arran agreed. "I'll do it. But I warn you. No Courtneys. No bores. And no little boys!"

Truiff looked hurt. "Arran—the little boy was five loops ago!"

"I can remember every moment of it," Arran said. "He came without an instruction booklet. What the hell do I do with a seven-year-old boy?"

"And it was your best acting up to then. Arran, I can't help it—I have to spring surprises on you. That's when you're at your best—dealing with difficulty. That's why you're an artist. That's why you're a legend."

"That's why you're rich," Arran pointed out, and then she walked quickly away, heading for the Sleeproom. Her eligibility began in half an hour, and every waking moment beyond that was a moment less of life.

Truiff followed her as far as she could, giving last-minute instructions on what to do when she woke, what to expect in the Sleeproom, how the instructions would be given to her in a way that she couldn't miss, but that the audience watching the holos wouldn't notice, and finally Arran made it through the door into the tape-and-tap, and Truiff had to stay behind.

Gentle and deferent attendants led her to the plush chair where the sleep helmet waited. Arran sighed and sat down, let the helmet slip onto her head, and tried to think happy thoughts as the tapes took her brain pattern—all her memories, all her personality—and recorded it to restore her at waking. What it was done, she got up and lazily walked to the table, shedding her robe on the way. She lay down with a groan of relief, and leaned her head back, surprised that the table, which looked so hard, could be soft.

It occurred to her (it always had before too, but she didn't know it) that she must have done this same thing twenty-two times before, because she had used somec that many times. But since the somec wiped clean all the brain activities during the sleep, including memory, she could never remember anything that happened to her after the taping. Funny. They could have her make love to all the attendants in the Sleeproom and she'd never know it.

But no, she realized as the sweet and deferent men and women soothingly wheeled the table to a place where monitoring instruments waited for her, no, that could never happen. The Sleeproom is the one place where no jokes are played, where nothing surprising or outrageous is ever done. Something in the world must be secure.

Then she giggled. Until my next waking, that is. And then the Sleeproom will be open to all the billions of poor suckers in the Empire who never get a chance at the somec, who have to live out their measly hundred years all in a row, while sleepers skip through the centuries like stones on a lake, touching down every few years.

And then the sweet young man with the daring cleft chin (pretty enough to be an actor, Arran noticed) pushed a needle gently into her arm, apologizing softly for the pain.

"That's all right, " Arran started to say, but then she felt a sharp pain in her arm, that spread quick as a fire to every part of her body; a terrible agony of heat that made her sweat leap from her pores. She cried out in pain and surprise—what was happening? Were they killing her? Who could want her to die?

And then the somec penetrated to her brain and ended all consciousness and all memory, including the memory of the pain that she had just felt. And when she woke again she would remember nothing of the agony of the somec. It would always and forever be a surprise.

◆ ◆ ◆

Truiff got the seven thousand eight hundred copies of the latest loop finished—most of them edited versions that cut out all sleeping hours and bodily functions other than eating and sex, the small minority full loops that truly dedicated (and rich) Arran Handully fans could view in small, private, seventeen-day-long showings. There were fans (crazy people, Truiff had long since decided, but thank Mother for them) who actually leased private copies of the unedited loops and watched them twice through on a single waking. That was one hell of a dedicated fan.

Once the loops were turned over to the distributors (and the advance money was paid in to Arran Handully Corporation credit accounts), Truiff went to the Sleeproom herself. It was the price of being a manager—up weeks before the star, back under somec weeks after. Truiff would die centuries before Arran. But Truiff was very philosophical about it. After all, she kept reminding herself, she might have a been a schoolteacher and never had somec at all.

◆ ◆ ◆

Arran woke sweating. Like every other sleeper, she believed that the perspiration was caused by the wake-up drugs, never suspecting that she was in that discomfort for the five years of sleep that had just passed. Her memories were intact, having been played back into her head only a few moments before. And she immediately realized that something was fastened to her right thigh—the loop recorder. She was already being taped, along with the room around her. For a brief moment she rebelled, regretting her decision to go along with the scheme. How could she bear to stay in character for the whole three weeks?

But the unbearable rule among lifeloop actors was "The loop never stops." No matter what you do, it's being looped, and there was no way to edit a loop. If there was one thing—one tiny thing—that had to be edited out in mid-action, the loop could simply be thrown away. The dedicated fans wouldn't stand for a loop that jumped from one scene to another—they were always sure that something juicy was being left out.

And so, almost by reflex, she composed herself into the tragically beautiful, sweet-souled yet bitter-tongued Arran Handully that all the fans knew and loved and paid money to watch. She sighed, and the sigh was seductive. She shuddered from the cold air passing across her sweating body, and turned the shiver into an excuse to open her eyes, blinking them delicately (seductively) against the dazzling lights.

And then she got up slowly, looked around. One of the ubiquitous attendants was standing nearby with a robe; Arran let him help her put it on, moving her shoulder just *so* in a way that made her breast rise just *that* much (never let it jiggle, nothing uglier that jiggling flesh, she reminded herself); and then she stepped to the newsboards. A quick flash through interplanetary news, and then a close study of Capitol events for the last five years, updating herself on who had done what to whom. And then she glanced at the game reports. Usually she only flipped a few pages and read virtually nothing—the games bored her—but this time she looked at it carefully for several minutes, pursing her lips and making a point of seeming to be dismayed or excited about individual game outcomes.

Actually, of course, she was reading the schedule for the next twenty-one days. Some of the names were new to her, of course—actors and actresses who were just reaching a level where they could afford to pay to be in an Arran Handully loop. And there were other names that she was quite familiar with, characters her fans would be expecting. Doret, her close friend and roommate seven loops ago, who still came back now and then to catch up on the news; Twern, that seven-year-old boy, now nearly fifteen, one of the youngest people ever to go on somec; old lovers. Which ones would be catty, and which ones would want to make up? Ah, well, she told herself. Plenty of chances to find that out.

A name far down on the list leapt out at her. Hamilton Ferlock! Involuntarily she smiled—caught herself in the sincere reaction and then decided that it would do no harm—the Arran Handully character might smile in just that way over a particular victory in a game. Hamilton Ferlock. Probably the one male actor on Capitol who could be considered to be in her class. They had started out at the same time too, and he had been her lover in her first five loops, back when she only had a few months on somec between wakings. And now he was gong to be in *this* loop!

She thought a silent blessing for her manager. Truiff had actually done something thoughtful.

And then it was the time to dress and leave the Sleeproom and walk the long corridors to her flat. She noticed as she walked along that the corridor had been redecorated, to give the illusion that somehow even the halls she walked along had class. She touched one of her new panels. Plastic. She refrained from grimacing. Oh well, the audience will never know it isn't really wood, and it keeps the overhead down.

She opened the door of her flat, and Doret screamed in delight and ran to embrace her. Arran decided that this time she should act a little put out at Doret for some imagined slight. Doret looked a little surprised, backed away, and then, like the consummate actress that she was (Arran didn't mind admitting the talents of her co-workers), she took Arran's quite subtle cue and turned it into a beautiful scene, Doret weeping out a confession that she had stolen a lover away from Arran several wakings ago, and Arran at first seeming to punish her, then forgiving. They ended the scene tearfully in each other's arms, and then paused a moment. Dammit, Arran thought. Truiff is at it again. Nobody entered to break the scene. They had to go on after the climax, which meant building it to an even bigger climax within the next three hours.

Arran was exhausted when Doret finally left. They had had a wrestling match, in which they had ripped each other's clothes to shreds, and finally Doret had pulled a knife on Arran. It was not until Arran managed to get the weapon away from her that Doret finally left, and Arran had a chance to relax for a moment.

Twenty-one days without a break, Arran reminded herself. And Truiff forcing me into exhaustion the first day. I'll fire the bitch, she vowed.

It was the twentieth day, and Arran was sick of the whole thing. Five parties, and a couple of orgies, and sleeping with someone new every night can pall rather quickly, and she had run the gamut of emotion several times. Each time she wept, she tried to put a different edge on it—tried to improvise new things to say to lovers, to shout in an argument, to use to insult a condescending visitor.

Most of her guests this time had been talented, and Arran certainly hadn't had to pull the full weight all by herself. But it was grueling, all the same.

And the buzzer sounded, and Arran had to get up to answer the door.

Hamilton Ferlock stood there, looking a little unsure of himself. Five centuries of acting, Arran thought to herself, and he still hasn't lost that ingenuous, boyish manner. She cried out his name (seductively, in character) and threw her arms around him.

"Ham," she said, "Oh, Ham, you wouldn't believe this waking! I'm so tired."

"Arran," he said softly, and Arran noticed with surprise that he was starting out sounding as if he loved her. Oh no, she thought. Didn't we part with a quarrel the last time? No, no, that was Ryden. Ham left because, because—oh, yes. Because he was feeling unfulfilled.

"Well, did you find what you are looking for?"

Ham raised an eyebrow. "Looking for?"

"You said you had to do something important with your life. That living with me was turning you into a lovesick shadow." Good phrase, Arran congratulated herself.

"Lovesick shadow. Well, you see, that was true enough," Ham answered. "But I've discovered that shadows only exist where there is light. You're my light, Arran, and only when I'm near you do I really exist."

No wonder he's so highly paid, Arran thought. The line was a bit gooey, but it's men like him who keep the women watching.

"Am I a light?" Arran said. "To think you've come back to me after so long."

"Like a moth to a flame."

And then, as was obligatory in all happy reunion scenes (have I already done a happy reunion in this waking? No) they slowly undressed each other and made love slowly, the kind of copulation that was not so much arousing as emotional, the kind that made both men and women cry and hold each other's hands in the theatre. He was so gentle this time, and the lovemaking was so right, that Arran felt hard-pressed to stay in character. I'm tired, she told herself. How can he carry it off so perfectly? He's a better actor than I remembered.

Afterward, he held her in his arms as they talked softly—he was always willing to talk afterward, unlike most actors, who thought they had to become surly after sex in order to maintain their macho image with fans.

"That was beautiful," Arran said, and she noticed with alarm that she wasn't acting. Watch yourself, woman. Don't screw up the loop after you've already invested twenty damned days.

"Was it?" Ham asked.

"Didn't you notice?"

He smiled. "After all these years, Arran, and I was right. There's no woman in the world worth loving with you around."

She giggled softly and ducked her head away from him in embarrassment. It was in character, and therefore seductive.

"Then why haven't you come back before?" Arran asked.

And Hamilton rolled over and lay on his back. Because he was silent for a few moments, she rubbed her fingers up and down his stomach. He smiled. "I stayed away, Arran, because I love you too much."

"Love is never a reason to stay away," she said. Ha. Let the fans quote *that* piece of crap for a couple of years.

"It is," Ham said, "when it's real."

"Even more reason to stay with me!" Arran put on a pout. "You left me, and now you pretend you loved me."

And suddenly Hamilton swung over and sat on the edge of the bed.

"What's wrong?" she asked.

"Damn!" he said. "Forget the stupid act, will you?"

"Act?"

"The damn Arran Handully character you're wearing for fun and profit! I know you, Arran, and I'm telling you—*I'm* telling you, not some actor, *me*—I'm telling you that I love you! Not for the audiences! Not for the loops! For you—I love *you*!"

And with a sickening feeling in the pit of her stomach Arran realized that, somehow, that stinking Truiff had gotten Ham to be a dirty trick after all. It was the one unspoken rule in the business—you never, never, never mention the fact that you're acting. For any reason. And now, the ultimate challenge—admitting to the audience that you're an actress and making them still believe you.

"Not for the loop!" she echoed back, struggling to think of some kind of answer.

"I said not for the loop!" He stood up and walked away from her, then turned back, pointed at her. "All these stupid affairs, all the phony relationships. Haven't you had enough?"

"Enough? This is life, and I'll never have enough of life."

But Ham was determined not to play fair.

"If this is life, Capital's an asteroid." A clumsy line, not like him. "Do you know what life is, Arran? Life is centuries playing loop after loop, as I've done, screwing every actress who can raise a fee, all so I can make enough money to buy somec and the luxuries of life. And all of a sudden a few years ago, I realized that the luxuries didn't mean a damn thing, and what did I care if I loved forever? Life was so utterly meaningless, just a succession of high-paid tarts!"

Arran managed to squeeze out some tears of rage. The loop never stops. "Are you calling *me* a tart?"

"You?" Ham looked absolutely stricken. The man can act, Arran reminded herself, even as she cursed him for throwing her such a rotten curve. "Not you, Arran, don't even think it!"

"What can I think with you coming here and accusing me of being a phony!"

"No," he said, sitting beside her on the bed again, putting his arm around her bare shoulder. She nestled to him again, as she had a dozen time before, years ago. She looked up at his face, and saw that his eyes were filled with tears.

"Why are you—why are you crying?" she asked, hesitantly.

"I'm crying for us," he said.

"Why?" she asked. "What do we have to cry over?"

"All the years we've lost."

"I don't know about *you*, but my years have been pretty full," she said, laughing, hoping he would laugh, too.

He didn't. "We were right for each other. Not just a team of actors, Arran, but as people. You weren't very good back then at the beginning—neither was I. I've looked at the loops. When we were with other people, we were as phony as two-bit beginners. But those loops still sold, made us rich, gave us a chance to learn the trade. Do you know why?"

"I don't agree with your assessment of the past," Arran said coldly, wondering what the hell he was trying to accomplish by continuing to refer to the loops instead of staying in character properly.

"We sold those tapes because of each other. Because we actually looked real when we told each other we loved, when we chattered for hours about nothing. We really enjoyed each other's company."

"I wish I were enjoying your company now. Telling me I'm a phony and that I have no talent."

"Talent! What a joke," Ham said. He touched her cheek, gently, turning her face so she would look at him. "Of course you have talent, and so have I.

We have money too and fame, and everything money can buy. Even friends. But tell me, Arran, how long has it been since you really loved anybody?"

Arran thought back through her most recent lovers. Any she wanted to make Ham's character jealous over? No. "I don't think I've ever really loved anybody."

"That's not true," Ham said. "It's not true, you loved me. Centuries ago, Arran, you truly loved me."

"Perhaps," she said. "But what does it have to do with now?"

"Don't you love me now?" Ham asked, and he looked so sincerely concerned that Arran was tempted to break character and laugh with delight, applaud his excellent performance. But the bastard was still making it hard for her, and so she decided to make it hard for him.

"Love you now?" she asked. "You're just another pair of eager gonads, my friend." That'd shock the fans. And, she hoped, completely mess up Ham's nasty little joke.

But Ham stayed right in character. He looked hurt, pulled away from her. "I'm sorry," he said. "I guess I was wrong." And to Arran's shock he began to dress.

"What are you doing?" she asked.

"Leaving," he said.

Leaving, Arran thought with panic. Leaving now? Without letting the scene have a climax? All this buildup, all the shattered traditions, and then leaving without a climax? The man was a monster!

"You can't go!"

"I was wrong. I'm sorry. I've embarrassed myself," he said.

"No, no, Ham, don't leave. I haven't seen you in so long!"

"You've never seen me," he answered. "Or you wouldn't have been capable of saying what you just did."

Making me pay for throwing a curve back at him, Arran thought. I'd like to kill him. What a fantastic actor, though. "I'm sorry I said it," Arran said, wearing contrition as if she had been dipped in it. "Forgive me. I didn't mean it."

"You just want me to stay so I won't ruin your damn scene."

Arran gave up in despair. Why am I doing this anyway? But the realization that breaking character now would wreck the whole loop kept her going. She went and threw herself on the bed. "That's right!" she said weeping. "Leave me now, when I want you so much."

Silence. She just lay there. Let him react.

But he said nothing. Just let the pause hang. She couldn't even hear him move.

Finally he spoke. "Do you mean it?"

"Mmm-hmm," she said, managing to hiccough through her tears. A cliché, but it got 'em every time.

"Not as an actress, Arran, please. As yourself. Do you love me? Do you want me?"

She rolled partway onto her side, lifted herself on one elbow, and said, the tears forcing a little catch in her voice, "I need you like I need somec, Ham. Why have you stayed away so long?"

He looked relieved. He walked slowly back to her. And everything was peaceful again. They made love four more times, between each of the courses of dinner, and for variety they let the servants watch. I've done it once before, Arran remembered, but it was five loops ago, about, and these are different servants anyway. Of course the servants, underpaid beginning actors all, used it as an excuse to get some interesting onstage time, and turned it into an orgy among themselves, managing every conceivable sexual act in only an hour and a half. Arran barely noticed them, though. They were the kind of fools who thought the audience wanted quantity. If some sex is good, a lot is better, they think. Arran knew better. Tease them. Let them beg. Let them find beauty in it too, not just titillation, not just lust. That's why she was a star, and they were playing servants in somebody else's loop.

That night Ham and Arran slept in each other's arms.

And in the morning Arran woke to find Ham staring at her, his face an odd mixture of love and pain. "Ham," she said softly, stroking his check. "What do you want?"

The longing in his face only increased. "Marry me," he said softly.

"Do you really mean it?" she asked, in her little-girl voice.

"I mean it. Time our wakings together, always."

"Always is a long time," she said. It was a good all-purpose line.

"And I mean it," he said. "Marry me. Mother knows we've made enough money over the years . We don't ever have to let these other bastards into our lives again. We don't ever have to wear these damned loop recorders again." And as he said that, he patted the recorder strapped to her thigh.

Arran inwardly groaned. He wasn't through with the games yet. Of course the audience wouldn't know what he meant—the computer that created the loop from the loop recorder was programmed to delete the recorder itself from the holo. The audience never saw it. And now Ham was referring to it. What was he trying to do, give her a nervous breakdown? Some friend.

Well, I can play his game. "I won't marry you," she said.

"Please," he said. "Don't you see how I love you? Do you think any of these phonies who pay to make love to you will ever feel one shred of real emotion toward you? To them you're a chance to make money, to make a name for themselves, to strike it rich. But I don't need money. I have a name. All I want is you. And all I can give you is me."

"Sweet," she said coldly, and got up and went into the kitchen. The clock said eleven-thirty. They had slept late. She was relieved. At noon she had to leave to get to the Sleeproom. In a half hour this farce would be over. Now to build it to a climax.

"Arran," Ham said, following her. "Arran, I'm serious, I'm not in character!"

That much is obvious, Arran thought but did not say.

"You're a liar," she said rudely.

He looked puzzled. "Why should I lie? Haven't I made it plain to you that I'm telling the truth? That I'm not acting?"

"Not acting," she said, sneering (but seductively, seductively. Never out of character, she reminded herself), and she turned her back on him. "Not acting. Well, as long as we're being honest about things, and throwing away both pretense and art, I'll play it your way, too. Do you know what I think of you?"

"What?" he asked.

"I think this is the cheapest, dirtiest trick I've ever seen. Coming here like this, doing everything you could to lead me into thinking you loved me, when all the time you were just exploiting me. Worse than all the others! You're the worst!"

He looked stricken. "I'd never exploit you!" he said.

"Marry me!" Arran laughed, mocking me. "Marry me, says you, and then what? What if this poor little girl actually did marry you? What would you do? Force me to stay in this flat forever? Keep away all my other friends, all my other—yes, even my lovers, you'd make me give them all up! Hundreds of men love me, but you, Hamilton, you want to own me forever, exclusively! What a coup that would be, wouldn't it? No one would ever get to look at my body again," she said, moving her body in such a way that on one else in the world could possibly want to look anywhere else, "except you. And you say you don't want to exploit me."

Hamilton came closer to her, tried to touch her, tried to plead with her, but she only grew angry, cursed him. "Stay away from me!" she screamed.

"Arran, you can't mean it," Ham said softly.

"I have never meant anything more thoroughly in my life," she said.

He looked in her eyes, looked deep. And finally he spoke again. "Either you're so much an actress that the real Arran Handully is lost, or you really do mean that. And either way, there's nothing for me to stay here for." And Arran watched admiringly as Hamilton gathered up his clothing and, not even bothering to dress, he left, closing the door quietly behind him. A beautiful exit, Arran thought. A lesser actor couldn't have resisted the temptation to say one last line. But not Ham—and now, if Arran played it right, this grotesque scene could be, after all, a genuine climax to the loop.

And so she played the scene, at first muttering about what a terrible man Ham was, and then progressing quickly to wondering whether he'd ever come back. "I hope he does," she said, and soon was weeping, crying out that she couldn't live without him. "Please come back, Ham!" she said pitifully. "I'm sorry I refused you! I *want* to marry you."

But then she looked at the clock. Nearly noon. Thank Mother. "But it's time," she said. "Time to go to the Sleeproom. The Sleeproom!" New hope came into her voice. That's it! I'll go the Sleeproom! I'll let the years pass by, and when I wake, there he'll be, waiting for me! She rhapsodized for a few more minutes, then threw a robe around herself and ran lightly, eagerly down the corridors to the Sleeproom.

In the tape-and-tap she chattered gaily to the attendant. "He'll be there waiting for me," she said, smiling. "Everything will be all right." The sleep helmet went on, and Arran kept talking. "You do think there's hope for me, don't you?" she asked, and the woman whose soft hands were now removing the helmet answered, "There's always hope, ma'am. Everybody has hope."

Arran smiled, then got up and walked briskly to the sleep table. She didn't remember ever doing this before, though she knew she must have—and then it occurred to her that *this* time she could watch the actual loop, see what really happened to her when the somec entered her veins.

But because she didn't remember any other administration of somec, she didn't realize the difference when the attendant gently put a needle only a millimeter under the surface of the palm of her hand. "It's so sharp," Arran said, "but I'm glad it doesn't hurt." And instead of the hot pain of somec, a gentle drowsiness filled her, and she was whispering Ham's name as she drifted off to sleep. Whispering his name, but silently cursing him under her breath. He may be a great actor, she told herself, but I ought to kick his head through a garbage chute for giving me a rotten time like that. Oh well. It'll sell seats in the theaters. Yawn. And then she slept.

The loop continued for a few more minutes, as the attendant went through a mumbo jumbo of nonsensical, meaningless activities. And finally they stepped back as if they were through, Arran's nude body lying on the table. Pause for the loop recorder to take the ending, and then:

A buzzer, and the door opened and Truiff came in, laughing in glee. "What a loop," she said, as she unstrapped the recorder from Arran's leg.

When Truiff had gone, the attendants put the real needle in Arran's arm, and the heat poured through her veins. Asleep though she had already been, Arran cried out in agony, and the sweat drenched the table in only a few minutes. It was ugly, painful, frightening. It just wouldn't do to have the masses see what somec was *really* like. Let them think the sleep is gentle; let them think the dreams are sweet.

When Arran woke, her first thought was to find out if the loop had *worked*. She had certainly gone through enough effort—now to see if Truiff's predictions of retirement had been fulfilled.

They had been.

Truiff was waiting right outside the Sleeproom, and hugged Arran tightly. "Arran, you wouldn't believe it!" she said, laughing uproariously. "Your last three loops had already set records—the highest-grossing loops of all time. But this one! This one!"

"Well?" Arran demanded.

"More than three times the total of those three loops put together!"

Arran smiled. "Then I can retire?"

"Only if you want to," Truiff said. "I have several pretty good deals worked out—"

"Forget it," Arran said.

"They wouldn't take much work, only a few days each—"

"I said forget it. From now on I never strap another recorder to my leg again. I'll guest. But I won't record."

"Fine, fine," Truiff said. "I told them, but they made me promise to ask you anyway."

"And probably paid you a pretty penny, too," Arran answered. Truiff shrugged and smiled.

"You're the greatest ever," Truiff said. "No one has ever done as well as you."

Arran shook her head. "Might be true," she said, "but I was really sweating it. That was a rotten trick you pulled on me, having Ham break character like that."

Truiff shook her head. "No, no, not at all, Arran. That must have been *his* idea. I told him to threaten to kill you—a real climax, you know. And then he went in and did what he did. Well, no harm done. It's an exquisite scene, and *because* he broke character and you, too there at the end—the audience believed that it *was* real. Beautiful. Of course, everybody and his duck is breaking character now, but it doesn't work anymore. Everyone knows it's just another device. But the first time, with you and Ham"—and Truiff made an expensive gesture—"it was magnificent."

Arran led the way down the corridor. "Well, I'm glad it worked. But I'm still looking forward to a chance to take Ham over the coals for it."

"Oh, Arran, I'm sorry," Truiff said.

Arran stopped and faced her manager. "For what?"

Truiff actually looked sad. "Arran, it's Hamilton. Not even a week after you went under—and it was the saddest thing. Everyone talked about it for days."

"What? Did something happen to him?"

"He hung himself. Turned off the lights in his flat so none of the Watchers could see him, and hung himself from a light fixture with a bathrobe tie. He died right away, no chance to revive him. It was terrible."

Arran was surprised to find a lump in her throat. A real one. "Ham's dead," she said softly. She remembered all the scenes they had played together, and a real fondness for him came over her. I'm not even acting, she realized. I truly cared for the man. Sweet, wonderful Ham.

"Does anyone know why he did it?" Arran asked.

Truiff shook her head. "No one has the slightest idea. And the thing I just can't believe—there it was, a scene they've never had before in a loop, a real suicide. And he didn't even record it!"

AFTERWORD TO "LIFELOOP"

by Orson Scott Card

Given how much of my life has been spent acting, directing, and writing (not to mention designing and building sets and costumes, doing makeup for, and spending ridiculous amounts of money funding) plays, it ought to be surprising that I have so rarely had any of my characters in any of my fiction be actors.

I had a little troupe of actors involved in the early volumes of the *Homecoming* series. I think I remember an actor or two in *Wyrms*.

And then there's "Lifeloop."

This story was written during the first year that I was selling fiction to Ben Bova at *Analog*. It arose out of one of the bull sessions I had with my friends and fellow writers, Jay Parry and Lane Johnson, both editors (along with me) at the *Ensign* magazine in Salt Lake City.

The premise was a simple one: What if you had soap operas where you pretended that the actors weren't actors at all? What if the show went on twenty-four hours a day, showing every aspect of the characters' lives? If your whole life was spent in performance, then…could you ever step outside of the performance, even when your whole future depended on it?

There is nothing about this idea to make it sci-fi—not today, anyway, in the era of "reality shows" that are anything but. (Nobody forgets the camera; even when they're not professional actors, once the camera is switched on they *are* acting!)

But I was a sci-fi writer, and if I was going to be able to publish it, it would have to a sci-fi story. So I set the tale within the future universe that I had invented for the earliest Worthing stories—the world of Capitol, where rich and powerful people took somec and slept for years at a time in order to postpone the day of their death.

What I slathered onto the story like peanut butter, Aaron Johnston would peel off it like dead skin after a sunburn. It came away clean in his play, leaving only the core story—only much further developed.

This is one of the few stories I've written that I think cries out to be a television series.

In the meantime, though, it was also an *early* story of mine. And one of the things that novice writers do is to think that a character's suicide is an ending. Now, more experienced, I know that suicide is what you resort to *instead* of an ending. So that's another way that Aaron's play improves on the original.

Yet the heart of the story worked then and works now, for me at least: People playing a role have a hard time knowing when to cut the act and get real. Of course, actors are only used as a metaphor here. This is something regular people do in real life all the time. We spend our lives caught up in the roles we have learned to play in relationship to all the people around us. It is nearly impossible to step back from those roles and think about them and examine them and decide whether that is who we really want to be.

A SEPULCHRE OF SONGS

by Orson Scott Card

She was losing her mind during the rain. For four weeks it came down nearly every day, and the people at the Millard County Rest Home didn't take any of the patients outside. It bothered them all, of course, and made life especially hellish for the nurses, everyone complaining to them constantly and demanding to be entertained.

Elaine didn't demand entertainment, however. She never seemed to demand much of anything. But the rain hurt her worse than anyone. Perhaps because she was only fifteen, the only child in an institution devoted to adult misery. More likely because she depended more than most on the hours spent outside; certainly she took more pleasure from them. They would lift her into her chair, prop her up with pillows so her body would stay straight, and then race down the corridor to the glass doors, Elaine calling, "Faster, faster," as they pushed her until finally they were outside. They told me she never really said anything out there. Just sat quietly in her chair on the lawn, watching everything. And then later in the day they would wheel her back in.

I often saw her being wheeled in – early, because I was there, though she never complained about my visits' cutting into her hours outside. As I watched her being pushed toward the rest home, she would smile at me so exuberantly that my mind invented arms for her, waving madly to match her childishly delighted face; I imagined legs pumping, imagined her running across the grass, breasting the air like great waves. But there were the pillows where arms should be, keeping her from falling to the side, and the belt around her middle kept her from pitching forward, since she had no legs to balance with.

It rained four weeks, and I nearly lost her.

My job was one of the worst in the state, touring six rest homes in as many counties, visiting each of them every week. I "did therapy" wherever the rest home administrators thought therapy was needed. I never figured out how they decided – all the patients were mad to one degree or another, most with the helpless insanity of age, the rest with the anguish of the invalid and the crippled.

You don't end up as a state-employed therapist if you had much ability in college. I sometimes pretend that I didn't distinguish myself in graduate school because I marched to a different drummer. But I didn't. As one kind professor gently and brutally told me, I wasn't cut out for science. But I was sure I was cut out for the art of therapy. Ever since I comforted my mother during her final year of cancer I had believed I had a knack for helping people get straight in their minds. I was everybody's confidant.

Somehow I had never supposed, though, that I would end up trying to help the hopeless in a part of the state where even the healthy didn't have much to live for. Yet that's all I had the credentials for, and when I (so maturely) told myself I was over the initial disappointment, I made the best of it.

Elaine was the best of it.

◆ ◆ ◆

"Raining raining raining," was the greeting I got when I visited her on the third day of the wet spell.

"Don't I know it?" I said. "My hair's soaking wet."

"Wish mine was," Elaine answered.

"No, you don't. You'd get sick."

"Not me," she said.

"Well, Mr. Woodbury told me you're depressed. I'm supposed to make you happy."

"Make it stop raining."

"Do I look like God?"

"I thought maybe you were in disguise. *I'm* in disguise," she said. It was one of our regular games. "I'm really a large Texas armadillo who was granted one wish. I wished to be a human being. But there wasn't enough of the armadillo to make a full human being; so here I am." She smiled. I smiled back.

Actually, she had been five years old when an oil truck exploded right in front of her parents' car, killing both of them and blowing her arms and legs right off. That she survived was a miracle. That she had to keep on living was unimaginable cruelty. That she managed to be a reasonably happy person, a favorite of the nurses – that I don't understand in the least. Maybe it was because she had nothing else to do. There aren't many ways that a person with no arms or legs can kill herself.

"I want to go outside," she said, turning her head away from me to look out the window.

Outside wasn't much. A few trees, a lawn, and beyond that a fence, not to keep the inmates in but to keep out the seamier residents of a rather seamy town. But there were low hills in the distance, and the birds usually seemed cheerful. Now, of course, the rain had driven both birds and hills into hiding. There was no wind, and so the trees didn't even sway. The rain just came straight down.

"Outer space is like the rain," she said. "It sounds like that out there, just a low drizzling sound in the background of everything."

"Not really," I said. "There's no sound out there at all."

"How do *you* know?" she asked.

"There's no air. Can't be any sound without air."

She looked at my scornfully. "Just as I thought. You don't *really* know. You've never *been* there, have you?"

"Are you trying to pick a fight?"

She started to answer, caught herself, and nodded. "Damned rain."

"At least you don't have to drive in it," I said. But her eyes got wistful, and I knew I had taken the banter too far. "Hey," I said. "First clear day I'll take you out driving."

"It's hormones," she said.

"What's hormones?"

"I'm fifteen. It always bothered me when I had to stay in. But I want to scream. My muscles are all bunched up, my stomach is all tight, I want to go outside and *scream*. It's hormones."

"What about your friends?" I asked.

"Are you kidding? They're all out there, playing in the rain."

"*All* of them?"

"Except Grunty, of course. He'd dissolve."

"And where's Grunty?"

"In the freezer, of course."

"Someday the nurses are going to mistake him for ice cream and serve him to the guests."

She didn't smile. She just nodded, and I knew that I wasn't getting anywhere. She really was depressed.

I asked her whether she wanted something.

"No pills," she said. "They make me sleep all the time."

"If I gave you uppers, it would make you climb walls."

"Neat trick," she said.

"It's that strong. So do you want something to take your mind off the rain and these four ugly yellow walls?"

She shook her head. "I'm trying not to sleep."

"Why not?"

She just shook her head again. "Can't sleep. Can't let myself sleep too much."

I asked again.

"Because," she said, "I might not wake up." She said it rather sternly, and I knew I shouldn't ask anymore. She didn't often get impatient with me, but I knew this time I was coming perilously close to overstaying my welcome.

"Got to go," I said. "You *will* wake up." And then I left, and I didn't see her for a week, and to tell the truth I didn't think of her much that week, what with the rain and a suicide in Ford County that really got to me, since she was fairly young and had a lot to live for, in my opinion. She disagreed and won the argument the hard way.

Weekends I live in a trailer in Piedmont. I live alone. The place is spotlessly clean because cleaning is something I do religiously. Besides, I tell myself, I might want to bring a woman home with me one night. Some nights I even do, and some nights I even enjoy it, but I always get restless and irritable when they start trying to get me to change my work schedule or take them along to the motels I live in or, once only, get the trailer-park manager to let them into my trailer when I'm gone. To keep things cozy for me. I'm not interested in "cozy." This is probably because of my mother's death; her cancer and my responsibilities as housekeeper for my father probably explain why I am a neat housekeeper. Therapist, therap thyself. The days passed in rain and highways and depressing people depressed out of their minds; the nights passed in television and sandwiches and motel bedsheets at state expense; and then it was time to go to the Millard County Rest Home again, where Elaine was waiting. It was then that I thought of her and realized that the rain had been going on for more than a week, and the poor girl must be almost out of her mind. I bought a cassette of Copland conducting Copland. She insisted on cassettes, because they stopped. Eight-tracks went on and on until she couldn't think.

♦ ♦ ♦

"Where have you been?" she demanded.

"Locked in a cage by a cruel duke in Transylvania. It was only four feet high, suspended over a pond filled with crocodiles. I got out by picking the lock with my teeth. Luckily, the crocodiles weren't hungry. Where have *you* been?"

"I mean it. Don't you keep a schedule?"

"I'm right on my schedule, Elaine. This is Wednesday. I was here last Wednesday. This year Christmas falls on a Wednesday, and I'll be here on Christmas."

"It feels like a year."

"Only ten months. This Christmas. Elaine, you aren't being any fun."

She wasn't in the mood for fun. There were tears in her eyes. "I can't stand much more," she said.

"I'm sorry."

"I'm afraid."

And she *was* afraid. Her voice trembled.

"At night, and in the daytime, whenever I sleep. I'm just the right size."

"For what?"

"What do you mean?"

"You said you were just the right size."

"I did? Oh, I don't know what I meant. I'm going crazy. That's what you're here for, isn't it? To keep me sane. It's the rain. I can't do anything, I can't see anything, and all I can hear most of the time is the hissing of the rain."

"Like outer space," I said, remembering what she had said the last time.

She apparently didn't remember our discussion. She looked startled. "How did you know?" she asked.

"You told me."

"There isn't any sound in outer space," she said.

"Oh," I answered.

"There's no air out there."

"I knew that."

"Then why did you say, 'Oh, of course'? The engines. You can hear them all over the ship. It's a drone, all the time. That's just like the rain. Only after a while you can't hear it anymore. It becomes like silence. Anansa told me."

Another imaginary friend. Her file said that she had kept her imaginary friends long after most children give them up. That was why I had first been assigned to see her, to get rid of the friends. Grunty, the ice pig; Howard, the boy who beat up everybody; Sue Ann, who would bring her dolls and play with them for her, making them do what Elaine said for them to do; Fuchsia, who lived among the flowers and was only inches high. There were others. After a few sessions with her I saw that she knew that they weren't real. But they passed time for her. They stepped outside her body and did things she could never do. I felt they did her no harm at all, and destroying that imaginary world for her would only make her lonelier and more unhappy. She was sane, that was certain. And yet I kept seeing her, not entirely because I liked her so much. Partly because I wondered whether she had been pretending when she told me she knew her friends weren't real. Anansa was a new one.

"Who's Anansa?"

"Oh, you don't want to know." She didn't want to talk abut her; that was obvious.

"I want to know."

She turned away. "I can't make you go away, but I wish you would. When you get nosy."

"It's my job."

"Job!" She sounded contemptuous. "I see all of you, running around on your healthy legs, doing all your *jobs*."

What could I say to her? "It's how we stay alive," I said. "I do my best."

Then she got a strange look on her face; *I've got a secret*, she seemed to say, *and I want you to pry it out of me*. "Maybe I can get a job, too."

"Maybe," I said. I tried to think of something she could do.

"There's always music," she said.

I misunderstood. "There aren't any instruments you can play. That's the way it is." Dose of reality and all that.

"Don't be stupid."

"Okay. Never again."

"I meant that there's always the music. On my job."

"And what job is this?"

"Wouldn't you like to know?" she said, rolling her eyes mysteriously and turning toward the window. I imagined her as a normal fifteen-year-old girl. Ordinarily I would have interpreted this as flirting. But there was something else under all this. A feeling of desperation. She was right. I really would like to know. I made a rather logical guess. I put together the two secrets she was trying to get me to figure out today.

"What kind of job is Anansa going to give you?"

She looked at me, startled. "So it's true then."

"What's true?"

"It's so frightening. I keep telling myself it's a dream. But it isn't, is it?"

"What, Anansa?"

"You think she's just one of my friends, don't you. But they're not in my dreams, not like this. Anansa – "

"What about Anansa?"

"She sings to me. In my sleep."

My trained psychologists's mind immediately conjured up mother figures. "Of course," I said.

"She's in space, and she sings to me. You wouldn't believe the songs."

It reminded me. I pulled out the cassette I had bought for her.

"Thank you," she said.

"You're welcome. Want to hear it?"

She nodded. I put it on the cassette player. *Appalachian Spring*. She moved her head to the music. I imagined her as a dancer. She felt the music very well.

But after a few minutes she stopped moving and started to cry.

"It's not the same," she said.

"You've heard it before?"

"Turn it off. Turn it *off!*"

I turned it off. "Sorry," I said. "Thought you'd like it."

"Guilt, nothing but guilt," she said. "You always feel guilty, don't you?"

"Pretty nearly always," I admitted cheerfully. A lot of my patients threw psychological jargon in my face. Or soap-opera language.

"*I'm* sorry," she said. "It's just – it's just not the music. Not *the* music. Now that I've heard it, everything is so dark compared to it. Like the rain, all gray and heavy and dim, as if the composer is trying to see the hills but the rain is always in the way. For a few minutes I thought he was getting it right."

"Anansa's music?"

She nodded. "I know you don't believe me. But I hear her when I'm asleep. She tells me that's the only time she can communicate with me. It's not talking. It's all her songs. She's out there, in her starship, singing. And at night I hear her."

"Why you?"

"You mean, Why only me?" She laughed. "Because of what I am. You told me yourself. Because I can't run around, I live in my imagination. She says that the threads between minds are very thin and hard to hold. But mine she can hold, because I live completely in my mind. She holds on to me. When I go to sleep, I can't escape her now anymore at all."

"Escape? I thought you liked her."

"I don't know what I like. I like—I like the music. But Anansa wants me. She wants to have me—she wants to give me a job."

"What's the singing like?" When she said *job*, she trembled and closed up; I referred back to something that she had been willing to talk about, to keep the floundering conversation going.

"It's not like anything. She's there in space, and it's black, just the humming of the engines like the sound of rain, and she reaches into the dust out there and draws in the songs. She reaches out her—out her fingers, or her ears, I don't know; it isn't clear. She reaches out and draws in the dust and the songs and turns them into the music that I hear. It's powerful. She says it's her songs that drive her between the stars."

"Is she alone?"

Elaine nodded. "She wants me."

"Wants you. How can she have you, with you here and her out there?"

Elaine licked her lips. "I don't want to talk about it," she said in a way that told me she was on the verge of telling me.

"I wish you would. I really wish you'd tell me."

"She says—she says that she can take me. She says that if I can learn the songs, she can pull me out of my body and take me there and give me arms and legs and fingers and I can run and dance and—"

She broke down, crying.

I patted her on the only place that she permitted, her soft little belly. She refused to be hugged. I had tried it years before, and she had screamed at me to stop it. One of the nurses told me it was because her mother had always hugged her, and Elaine wanted to hug back. And couldn't.

"It's a lovely dream, Elaine."

"It's a terrible dream. Don't you see? I'll be like *her*."

"And what's she like?"

"She's the ship. She's the starship. And she wants me with her, to be the starship with her. And sing our way through space together for thousands and thousands of years."

"It's just a dream, Elaine. You don't have to be afraid of it."

"They did it to her. They cut off her arms and legs and put her into the machines."

"But no one's going to put you into a machine."

"I want to go outside," she said.

"You can't. It's raining."

"Damn the rain."

"I do, every day."

"I'm not joking! She pulls me all the time now, even when I'm awake. She keeps pulling at me and making me fall asleep, and she sings to me, and I feel her pulling and pulling. If I could just go outside, I could hold on. I feel like I could hold on, if I could just—"

"Hey, relax. Let me give you a—"

"No! I don't want to sleep!"

"Listen, Elaine. It's just a dream. You can't let it get to you like this. It's just the rain keeping you here. It makes you sleepy, and so you keep dreaming this. But don't fight it. It's a beautiful dream in a way. Why not go with it?"

She looked at me with terror in her eyes.

"You don't mean that. You don't want me to go."

"No. Of course I don't you to go anywhere. But you won't, don't you see? It's a dream, floating out there between the stars—"

"She's not floating. She's ramming her way through space so fast it makes me dizzy whenever she shows me."

"Then be dizzy. Think of it as your mind finding a way for you to run."

"You don't understand, Mr. Therapist. I thought you'd understand."

"I'm trying to."

"If I go with her, then I'll be dead."

◆ ◆ ◆

I asked her nurse, "Who's been reading to her?"

"We all do, and volunteers from town. They like her. She always has someone to read to her."

"You'd better supervise them more carefully. Somebody's been putting ideas in her head. About spaceships and dust and singing between the stars. It's scared her pretty bad."

The nurse frowned. "We approve everything they read. She's been reading that kind of thing for years. It's never done her any harm before. Why now?"

"The rain, I guess. Cooped up in here, she's losing touch with reality."

The nurse nodded sympathetically and said, "I know. When she's asleep, she's doing the strangest things now."

"Like what? What kind of things?"

"Oh, singing these horrible songs."

"What are the words?"

"There aren't any words. She just sort of hums. Only the melodies are awful. Not even like music. And her voice gets funny and raspy. She's completely asleep. She sleeps a lot now. Mercifully, I think. She's always gotten impatient when she can't go outside."

The nurse obviously liked Elaine. It would be hard not to feel sorry for her, but Elaine insisted on being liked, and people liked her, those that could get over the horrible flatness of the sheets all around her trunk. "Listen," I said. "Can we bundle her up or something? Get her outside in spite of the rain?"

The nurse shook her head. "It isn't just the rain. It's cold out there. And the explosion that made her like she is—it messed her up inside. She isn't put together right. She doesn't have the strength to fight off any kind of disease at all. You understand—there's a good chance that exposure to that kind of weather would kill her eventually. And I won't take a chance on that."

"I'm going to be visiting her more often, then," I said. "As often as I can. She's got something going on in her head that's scaring her half to death. She thinks she's going to die."

"Oh, the poor darling," the nurse said. "Why would she think that?"

"Doesn't matter. One of her imaginary friends may be getting out of hand."

"I thought you said they were harmless."

"They were."

When I left the Millard County Rest Home that night, I stopped back in Elaine's room. She was asleep, and I heard her song. It was eerie. I could hear, now and then, themes from the bit of Copland music she had listened to. But it was distorted, and most of the music was unrecognizable—wasn't even music. Her voice was high and strange, and then suddenly it would change, would become low and raspy, and for a moment I clearly heard in her voice the sound of a vast engine coming through walls of metal, carried on slender metal rods, the sound of a great roar being swallowed up by a vast cushion of nothing. I picture Elaine with wires coming out of her shoulders and hips, with her head encased in metal and her eyes closed in sleep, like her imaginary Anansa, piloting the starship as if it were her own body. I could see that this would be attractive to Elaine, in a way. After all, she hadn't been born this way. She had memories of running and playing, memories of feeding herself and dressing herself, perhaps even of learning to read, of sounding out the words as her fingers touched each letter. Even the false arms of a spaceship would be something to fill the great void.

Children's centers are not inside their bodies; their centers are outside, at the point where the fingers of the left hand and the fingers of the right hand meet. What they touch is where they live; what they see is their self. And Elaine had lost herself in an explosion before she had the chance to move inside. With this strange dream of Anansa she was getting a self back.

But a repellent self, for all that. I walked in and sat by Elaine's bed, listening to her sing. Her body moved slightly, her back arching a little with the melody. High and light; low and rasping. The sounds alternated, and I wondered what they meant. What was going on inside her to make this music come out?

If I go with her, then I'll be dead.

Of course she was afraid. I looked at the lump of flesh that filled the bed shapelessly below where her head emerged from the covers. I tried to change my perspective, to see her body as she saw it, from above. It almost disappeared then, with the foreshortening and the height of her ribs making her stomach and hint of hips vanish into insignificance. Yet this was all she had, and if she believed—and certainly she seemed to—that surrendering to the fantasy of Anansa would mean the death of this pitiful body, is death any less frightening to those who have not been able to fully live? I doubt it. At least for Elaine, what life she had lived had been joyful. She would not willingly trade it for a life of music and metal arms, locked in her own mind.

Except for the rain. Except that nothing was so read to her as the outside, as the trees and birds and distant hills, and as the breeze touching her with a violence she permitted to no living person. And with that reality, the good part of her life, cut off from her by the rain, how long could she hold out against the incessant pulling of Anansa and her promise of arms and legs and eternal song?

I reached up, on a whim, and very gently lifted her eyelids.

Her eyes remained open, staring at the ceiling, not blinking.

I closed her eyes, and they remained closed.

I turned her head, and it stayed turned. She did not wake up. Just kept singing as if I had done nothing to her at all.

Catatonia, or the beginning of catalepsy. *She's losing her mind*, I thought, *and if I don't bring her back, keep her here somehow, Anansa will win, and the rest home will be caring for a lump of mindless flesh for the next however many years they can keep this remnant of Elaine alive.*

"I'll be back on Saturday," I told the administrator.

"Why so soon?"

"Elaine is going through a crisis of some kind," I explained. An imaginary woman from space wants to carry her off—that I didn't say. "Have the nurses keep her awake as much as they can. Read to her, play with her, talk to her. Her normal hours at night are enough. Avoid naps."

"Why?"

"I'm afraid for her, that's all. She could go catatonic on us at any time, I think. Her sleeping isn't normal. I want to have her watched all the time."

"This is really serious?"

"This is really serious."

♦ ♦ ♦

On Friday it looked as if the clouds were breaking, but after only a few minutes of sunshine a huge new bank of clouds swept down from the northwest, and it was worse than before. I finished my work rather carelessly, stopping a sentence in the middle several times. One of my patients was annoyed with me. She squinted at me. "You're not paid to think about your woman troubles when you're talking to me." I apologized and tried to pay attention. She was a talker; my attention always wandered. But she was right in a way. I couldn't stop thinking of Elaine. And my patient's saying that about woman troubles must have triggered something in my mind. After all, my relationship with Elaine was the longest and closest I had had with a woman in many years. If you could think of Elaine as a woman.

On Saturday I drove back to Millard County and found the nurses rather distraught. They didn't realize how much she was sleeping until they tried to stop her, they all said. She was dozing off for two or three naps in the mornings, even more in the afternoons. She went to sleep at night at seven-thirty and slept at least twelve hours. "Singing all the time. It's awful. Even at night she keeps it up. Singing and singing."

But she was awake when I went in to see her.

"I stayed awake for you."

"Thanks," I said.

"A Saturday visit. I must really be going bonkers."

"Actually, no. But I don't like how sleepy you are."

She smiled wanly. "It isn't my idea."

I think my smile was more cheerful than hers. "And I think it's all in your head."

"Think what you like, Doctor."

"I'm not a doctor. My degree says I'm a master."

"How deep is the water outside?"

"Deep?"

"All this rain. Surely it's enough to keep a few dozen arks afloat. Is God destroying the world?"

"Unfortunately, no. Though He has killed the engines on a few cars that went a little fast through the puddles."

"How long would it have to rain to fill up the world?"

"The world is round. It would all drip off the bottom."

She laughed. It was good to hear her laugh, but it ended too abruptly, and she looked at me fearfully. "I'm going, you know."

"You are?"

"I'm just the right size. She's measured me, and I'll fit perfectly. She has just the place for me. It's a good place, where I can hear the music of the dust for myself, and learn to sing it. I'd have the directional engines."

I shook my head. "Grunty the ice pig was cute. This isn't cute, Elaine."

"Did I ever say I thought Anansa was cute? Grunty the ice pig was real, you know. My father made him out of crushed ice for a luau. He melted before they got the pig out of the ground. I don't make my friends up."

"Fuchsia the flower girl?"

"My mother would pinch blossoms off the fuchsia by our front door. We played with them like dolls in the grass."

"But not Anansa."

"Anansa came into my mind when I was asleep. She found me. I didn't make her up."

"Don't you see, Elaine, that's how the real hallucinations come? They feel like reality."

She shook her head. "I know all that. I've had the nurses read me psychology books. Anansa is—Anansa is other. She couldn't come out of my head. She's something else. She's real. I've heard her music. It isn't plain, like Copland. It isn't false."

"Elaine, when you were asleep on Wednesday, you were becoming catatonic."

"I know."

"You know?"

"I felt you touch me. I felt you turn my head. I wanted to speak to you, to say good-bye. But she was singing, don't you see? She was singing. And now she lets me sing along. When I sing with her, I can feel myself travel out, like a spider along a single thread, out into the place where she is. Into the darkness. It's lonely there, and black, and cold, but I know that at the end of the thread there she'll be, a friend for me forever."

"You're frightening me, Elaine."

"There aren't any trees on her starship, you know. That's how I stay here. I think of the trees and the hills and the birds and the grass and the wind, and how I'd lose all of that. She gets angry at me, and a little hurt. But it keeps me here. Except now I can hardly remember the trees at all. I try to remember, and it's like trying to remember the face of my mother. I can remember her dress and her hair, but her face is gone forever. Even when I look at a picture, it's a stranger. The trees are strangers to me now."

I stroked her forehead. At first she pulled away, then slid it back.

"I"m sorry," she said. "I usually don't like people to touch me there."

"I won't," I said.

"No, go ahead. I don't mind."

So I stroked her forehead again. It was cool and dry, and she lifted her head almost imperceptibly, to receive my touch. Involuntarily I thought of what the old woman had said the day before. *Woman troubles.* I was touching Elaine, and I thought of making love to her. I immediately put the thought out of my mind.

"Hold me here," she said. "Don't let me go. I want to go so badly. But I'm not meant for that. I'm just the right size, but not the right shape. Those aren't my arms. I know what my arms felt like."

"I'll hold you if I can. But you have to help."

"No drugs. The drugs pull my mind away from my body. If you give me drugs, I'll die."

"Then what can I do?"

"Just keep me here, any way you can."

Then we talked about nonsense, because we had been so serious, and it was as if she weren't having any problems at all. We got on the subject of the church meetings.

"I didn't know you were religious," I said.

"I'm not. But what else is there to do on Sunday? They sing hymns, and I sing with them. Last Sunday there was a sermon that really got to me. The preacher talked about Christ in the sepulchre. About Him being there three days before the angel came to let Him go. I've been thinking about that, what it must have been like for Him, locked in a cave of darkness, completely alone."

"Depressing."

"Not really. It must have been exhilarating for Him, in a way. If it was true, you know. To lie there on that stone bed, saying to Himself, 'They thought I was dead, but I'm here. I'm not dead.'"

"You make Him sound smug."

"Sure. Why not? I wonder if I'd feel like that, if I were with Anansa."

Anansa again.

"I can see what you're thinking. You're thinking, 'Anansa again.'"

"Yeah," I said. "I wish you'd erase her and go back to some more harmless friends."

Suddenly her face went angry and fierce.

"You can believe what you like. Just leave me alone."

I tried to apologize, but she wouldn't have any of it. She insisted on believing in this star woman. Finally I left, redoubling my cautions against letting her sleep. The nurses looked worried, too. They could see the change as easily as I could.

That night, because I was in Millard on a weekend, I called up Belinda. She wasn't married or anything at the moment. She came to my motel. We had dinner, made love, and watched television. She watched television, that is. I lay on the bed, thinking. And so when the test pattern came on and Belinda at last got up, beery and passionate, my mind was still on Elaine. As Belinda kissed and tickled me and whispered stupidity in my ear, I imagined myself without arms and legs. I lay there, moving only my head.

"What's the matter, you don't want to?"

I shook off the mood. No need to disappoint Belinda—I was the one who had called *her*. I had a responsibility. Not much of one, though. That was what was nagging at me. I made love to Belinda slowly and carefully, but with my eyes closed. I kept superimposing Elaine's face on Belinda's. Woman troubles. Even though Belinda's fingers played up and down my back, I thought I was making love to Elaine. And the stumps of arms and legs didn't revolt me as much as I would have thought. Instead, I only felt sad. A deep sense of tragedy, of loss, as if Elaine were dead and I could have saved her, like the prince in all the fairy tales; a kiss, so symbolic, and the princess awakens and lives happily ever after. And I hadn't done it. I had failed her. When we were finished, I cried.

"Oh, you poor sweetheart," Belinda said, her voice rich with sympathy. "What's wrong—you don't have to tell me." She cradled me for a while, and at last I went to sleep with my head pressed against her breasts. She thought I needed her. I suppose that, briefly, I did.

◆ ◆ ◆

I did not go back to Elaine on Sunday as I had planned. I spent the entire day almost going. Instead of walking out the door, I sat and watched the incredible array of terrible Sunday morning television. And when I finally did go out, fully intending to go to the rest home and see how she was doing, I ended up driving, luggage in the back of the car, to my trailer, where I went inside and again sat down and watched television.

Why couldn't I go to her?

Just keep me here, she had said. Any way you can, she had said.

And I thought I knew the way. That was the problem. In the back of my mind all this was much too real, and the fairy tales were wrong. The prince didn't wake her with a kiss. He wakened the princess with a promise: In his arms she would be safe forever. She awoke for the happily ever after. If she hadn't known it to be true, the princess would have preferred to sleep forever.

What was Elaine asking of me?

Why was I afraid of it?

Not my job. Unprofessional to get emotionally involved with a patient.

But then, when had I ever been a professional? I finally went to bed, wishing I had Belinda with me again, for whatever comfort she could bring. Why weren't all women like Belinda, soft and loving and undemanding?

Yet as I drifted off to sleep, it was Elaine I remembered, Elaine's face and hideous, reproachful stump of a body that followed me through all my dreams.

And she followed me when I was awake, through my regular rounds on Monday and Tuesday, and at last it was Wednesday, and still I was afraid to go to the Millard County Rest Home. I didn't get there until afternoon. Late afternoon, and the rain was coming down as hard as ever, and there were lakes of standing water in the fields, torrents rushing through the unprepared gutters of the town.

"You're late," the administrator said.

"Rain," I answered, and he nodded. But he looked worried.

"We hoped you'd come yesterday, but we couldn't reach you anywhere. It's Elaine."

And I knew that my delay had served its damnable purpose, exactly as I expected.

"She hasn't woken up since Monday morning. She just lies there, singing. We've got her on an IV. She's asleep."

She was indeed asleep. I sent the others out of the room.

"Elaine," I said.

Nothing.

I called her name again, several times. I touched her, rocked her head back and forth. Her head stayed where I placed it. And the song went on, softly, high and then low, pure and then gravelly. I covered her mouth. She sang on, even with her mouth closed, as if nothing were the matter.

I pulled down her sheet and pushed a pin into her belly, then into the thin flesh at her collarbone. No response. I slapped her face. No response. She was gone. I saw her again, connected to a starship, only this time I understood better. It wasn't her body that was the right size; it was her mind. And it was her mind that had followed the slender spider's thread out to Anansa, who waited to give her a body.

A job.

Shock therapy? I imagined her already-deformed body leaping and arching as the electricity coursed through her. It would accomplish nothing, except to torture unthinking flesh. Drugs? I couldn't think of any that could bring her back from where she had gone. In a way, I think, I even believed in Anansa, for the moment. I called her name. "Anansa, let her go. Let her come back to me. Please. I need her."

Why had I cried in Belinda's arms? Oh, yes. Because I had seen the princess and let her lie there unawakened, because the happily ever after was so damnably much work.

I did not do it in the fever of the first realization that I had lost her. It was no act of passion or sudden fear or grief. I sat beside her bed for hours, looking at her weak and helpless body, now so empty. I wished for her eyes to open on their own, for her to wake up and say, "Hey would you believe the dream *I* had!" For her to say, "Fooled you, didn't I? It was really hard when you poked me with pins, but I fooled you."

But she hadn't fooled me.

And so, finally, not with passion but in despair, I stood up and leaned over her, leaned my hands on either side of her and pressed my cheek against hers and whispered in her ear. I promised her everything I could think of. I promised her no more rain forever. I promised her trees and flowers and hills and birds and the wind for as long as she liked. I promised to take her away from the rest home, to take her to see things she could only have dreamed of before.

And then, at last, with my voice harsh from pleading with her, with her hair wet with my tears, I promised her the only thing that might bring her back. I promised her me. I promised her love forever stronger than any songs Anansa could sing.

And it was then that the monstrous song fell silent. She did not awaken, but the song ended, and she moved on her own; her head rocked to the side, and she seemed to sleep normally, not catatonically. I waited by her bedside all night. I fell asleep in the chair, and one of the nurses covered me. I was still there when I was awakened in the morning by Elaine's voice.

"What a liar you are! It's still raining."

♦ ♦ ♦

It was a feeling of power, to know that I had called someone back from places far darker than death. Her life was painful, and yet my promise of devotion was enough, apparently, to compensate. This was how I understood it, at least. This was what made me feel exhilarated, what kept me blind and deaf to what had really happened.

I was not the only one rejoicing. The nurses made a great fuss over her, and the administrator promised to write up a glowing report. "Publish," he said.

"It's too personal," I said. But in the back of my mind I was already trying to figure out a way to get the case into print, to gain something for my career. I was ashamed of myself for twisting what had been an honest, heartfelt commitment into personal advancement. But I couldn't ignore the sudden respect I was receiving from people to whom, only hours before, I had been merely ordinary.

"It's too personal," I repeated firmly. "I have no intention of publishing."

And to my disgust I found myself relishing the administrator's respect for that decision. There was no escape from my swelling self-satisfaction. Not as long as I stayed around those determined to give me cheap payoffs. Ever the wise psychologist, I returned to the only person who would give me gratitude instead of admiration. *The gratitude I had earned,* I thought. I went back to Elaine.

"Hi," she said. "I wondered where you had gone."

"Not far," I said. "Just visiting with the Nobel Prize committee."

"They want to reward you for bringing me here?"

"Oh, no. They had been planning to give me the award for having contacted a genuine alien being from outer space. Instead, I blew it and brought you back. They're quite upset."

She looked flustered. It wasn't like her to look flustered—usually she came back with another quip. "But what will they do to you?"

"Probably boil me in oil. That's the usual thing. Though, maybe they've found a way to boil me in solar energy. It's cheaper." A feeble joke. But she didn't get it.

"This isn't the way she said it was—she said it was—"

She. I tried to ignore the dull fear that suddenly churned in my stomach. *Be analytical,* I thought. *She could be anyone.*

"She said? Who said?" I asked.

Elaine fell silent. I reached out and touched her forehead. She was perspiring.

"What's wrong?" I asked. "You're upset."

"I should have known."

"Known what?"

She shook her head and turned away from me.

I knew what it was, I thought. I knew what it was, but we could surely cope. "Elaine," I said, "you aren't completely cured, are you? You haven't got rid of Anansa, have you? You don't have to hide it from me. Sure, I would have loved to think you'd been completely cured, but that would have been too much of a miracle. Do I look like a miracle worker? We've just made progress, that's all. Brought you back from catalepsy. We'll free you of Anansa eventually."

Still she was silent, staring at the rain-gray window.

"You don't have to be embarrassed about pretending to be completely cured. It was very kind of you. It made me feel very good for a little while. But I'm a grown-up. I can cope with a little disappointment. Besides, you're awake, you're back, and that's all that matters." Grown-up, hell! I was terribly disappointed, and ashamed that I wasn't more sincere in what I was saying. No cure after all. No hero. No magic. No great achievement. Just a psychologist who was, after all, not extraordinary.

But I refused to pay too much attention to those feelings. Be a professional, I told myself. She needs your help.

"So don't go feeling guilty about it."

She turned back to face me, her eyes full. "Guilty?" She almost smiled. "Guilty." Her eyes did not leave my face, though I doubted she could see me well through the tears brimming her lashes.

"You tried to do the right thing," I said.

"Did I? Did I really?" She smiled bitterly. It was a strange smile for her, and for a terrible moment she no longer looked like my Elaine, my bright young patient. "I meant to stay with her," she said. "I wanted her with me, she was so alive, and when she finally joined herself to the ship, she sang and danced and swung her arms, and I said, 'This is what I've needed; this is what I've craved all my centuries lost in the songs.' But then I heard *you*."

"Anansa," I said, realizing at that moment who was with me.

"I heard *you*, crying out to her. Do you think I made up my mind quickly? She heard you, but she wouldn't come. She wouldn't trade her new arms and legs for anything. They were so new. But I'd had them for long enough. What I'd never had was—you."

"Where is she?" I asked.

"Out there," she said. "She sings better than I ever did." She looked wistful for a moment, then smiled ruefully. "And I'm here. Only I made a bad bargain, didn't I? Because I didn't fool you. You don't want me, now. It's Elaine you want, and she's gone. I left her alone out there. She won't mind, not for a long time. But then—then she will. Then she'll know I cheated her."

The voice was Elaine's voice, the tragic little body her body. But now I knew I had not succeeded at all. Elaine was gone, in the infinite outer space where the mind hides to escape from itself. And in her place—Anansa. A stranger.

"You cheated her?" I said. "How did you cheat her?"

"It never changes. In a while you learn all the songs, and they never change. Nothing moves. You go on forever until all the stars fail, and yet nothing ever moves."

I moved my hand and put it to my hair. I was startled at my own trembling touch on my head.

"Oh, God," I said. They were just words, not a supplication.

"You hate me," she said.

Hate her? Hate my little, mad Elaine? Oh, no. I had another object for my hate. I hated the rain that had cut her off from all that kept her sane. I hated her parents for not leaving her home the day they let their car drive them on to death. But most of all I remembered my days of hiding from Elaine, my days of resisting her need, of pretending that I didn't remember her or think of her or need her, too. She must have wondered why I was so long in coming. Wondered and finally given up hope, finally realized that there was no one who would hold her. And so she left, and when I finally came, the only person waiting inside her body was Anansa, the imaginary friend who had come, terrifyingly, to life. I knew whom to hate. I thought I would cry. I even buried my face in the sheet where her leg would have been. But I did not cry. I just sat there, the sheet harsh against my face, hating myself.

Her voice was like a gentle hand, a pleading hand touching me. "I'd undo it if I could," she said. "But I can't. She's gone, and I'm here. I came because of you. I came to see the trees and the grass and the birds and your smile. The happily ever after. That was what she had lived for, you know, all she lived for. Please smile at me."

I felt warmth on my hair. I lifted my head. There was no rain in the window. Sunlight rose and fell on the wrinkles of the sheet.

"Let's go outside," I said.

"It stopped raining," she said.

"A bit late, isn't it?" I answered. But I smiled at her.

"You can call me Elaine," she said. "You won't tell, will you?"

I shook my head. No, I wouldn't tell. She was safe enough. I wouldn't tell because then they would take her away to a place where psychiatrists reigned but did not know enough to rule. I imagined her confined among others who had also made their escape from reality and I knew that I couldn't tell anyone. I also knew I couldn't confess failure, not now.

Besides, I hadn't really completely failed. There was still hope. Elaine wasn't really gone. She was still there, hidden in her own mind, looking out through this imaginary person she had created to take her place. Someday I would find her and bring her home. After all, even Grunty the ice pig had melted.

I noticed that she was shaking her head. "You won't find her," she said. "You won't bring her home. I won't melt and disappear. She *is* gone and you couldn't have prevented it."

I smiled. "Elaine," I said.

And then I realized that she had answered thoughts I hadn't put into words.

"That's right," she said, "Let's be honest with each other. You might as well. You can't lie to me."

I shook my head. For a moment, in my confusion and despair, I had believed it all, believed that Anansa was real. But that was nonsense. Of course Elaine knew what I was thinking. She knew me better than I knew myself.

"Let's go outside," I said. A failure and a cripple, out to enjoy the sunlight, which fell equally on the just and the unjustifiable.

"I don't mind," she said. "Whatever you want to believe: Elaine or Anansa. Maybe it's better if you still look for Elaine. Maybe it's better if you let me fool you after all."

The worst thing about the fantasies of the mentally ill is that they're so damned consistent. They never let up. They never give you any rest.

"I'm Elaine," she said, smiling. "I'm Elaine, pretending to be Anansa. You love me. That's what I came for. You promised to bring me home, and you did. Take me outside. You made it stop raining for me. You did everything you promised, and I'm home again, and I promise I'll never leave you."

She hasn't left me. I come to see her every Wednesday as part of my work, and every Saturday and Sunday as the best part of my life. I take her driving with me sometimes, and we talk constantly, and I read to her and bring her books for the nurses to read to her. None of them know that she is still unwell—to them she's Elaine, happier than ever, pathetically delighted at every sight and sound and smell and taste and every texture that they touch against her cheek. Only *I* know that I have made no progress at all since then, that in moments of terrible honesty I call her Anansa, and she sadly answers me.

But in a way I'm content. Very little has changed between us, really. And after a few weeks I realized, with certainty, that she was happier now than she had ever been before. After all, she had the best of all possible worlds, for her. She could tell herself that the real Elaine was off in space somewhere, dancing and singing and hearing songs, with arms and legs at last, while the poor girl who was confined to this limbless body at the Millard County Rest Home was really an alien who was very, very happy to have even that limited body.

And as for me, I kept my commitment to her, and I'm happier for it. I'm still human—I still take another woman into my bed from time to time. But Anansa doesn't mind. She even suggested it, only a few days after she woke up. "Go back to Belinda sometimes," she said. "Belinda loves you, too, you know. I won't mind at all." I still can't remember when I spoke to her of Belinda, but at least she didn't mind, and so there aren't really any discontentments in my life. Except.

Except that I'm not God. I would like to be God. I would make some changes.

When I go to the Millard County Rest Home, I never enter the building first. She is never in the building. I walk around the outside and look across the lawn by the trees. The wheelchair is always there; I can tell it from the others by the pillows, which glare white in the sunlight. I never call out. In a few moments she always sees me, and the nurses wheel her around and push the chair across the lawn.

She comes as she has come hundreds of times before. She plunges toward me, and I concentrate on watching her, so that my mind will not see my Elaine surrounded by blackness, plunging through space, gathering dust, gathering songs, leaping and dancing with her new arms and legs that she loves better than me. Instead I watch the wheelchair, watch the smile on her face. She's happy to see me, so delighted with the world outside that her body cannot contain her. And when my imagination will not be restrained, I am God for a moment. I see her running toward me, her arms waving. I give her a left hand, a right hand, delicate and strong; I put a long and girlish left leg on her, and one just as sturdy on the right.

And then, one by one, I take them all away.

AFTERWORD TO "SEPULCHRE"

by Orson Scott Card

"A Sepulchre of Songs" was written a long time ago, out of my imagination. My wife and I were living in a rented house at 117 J Street in Salt Lake City, and our first child was an infant. I was just at the beginning of my career as a fiction writer, and most of our income actually came from audioscripts I was writing for Living Scriptures in Ogden, Utah.

The idea for this story arose out of an old science fiction tradition: mechanical people wishing to be human. As I first conceived of it, Anansa was definitely a real person, cyborgized and controlling a starship out in space. Lacking a body, the ship itself had become her arms and legs and voice. But she was lonely and she longed to be a living organism again.

The irony of the story, then, would be that the only person with whom she could communicate and eventually trade "bodies" would be a young woman with no arms and legs. Yet to Anansa, that body would be better than what she had; and vice versa. It would be a fair trade.

The trouble was that as I wrote the story—from the point of view of the therapist sent to help cure her of the fantasies that kept the limbless girl sane—I began to realize that as far as the therapist knew, the "trade" might just as easily be entirely imaginary. And, without violating his point of view or the fundamental rules of the story, there was no way for the reader to be certain, either.

So regardless of the fact that the idea centered around Anansa, the story centered around the therapist who falls in love with Elaine and then can't tell whether she is still present in that body. The ambiguity became part of their relationship. Was he giving himself to a stranger? Was the girl he loved trapped in a spaceship now?

The answer doesn't actually matter, because the story is about what both Elaine and the therapist chose. Elaine chose to leave her present life—no matter how you interpret the story—despite how much she might have loved the therapist; while the therapist has chosen to sacrifice any chance of a normal relationship and devote his love and his life to this crippled young woman. My hope was that both choices would be completely understandable.

Since the writing of this story, though, my wife and I had a child—our third, named Charles Benjamin—who, while he had all his limbs, did not have the use of them. We spent seventeen years caring for a child who could not sit up or stand or walk or drink or eat without help. Not only that, we watched as other people chose to become involved with his life and serve him and love him along with us.

In other words, we knew that while most people are somewhat repelled by a crippled or deformed body, it was quite possible for others to love a child like this. We also watched as Charlie grew into his teens and became aware of the life he wanted but could never have: The girls he had crushes on, but could never speak to, because—unlike Elaine in my story—Charlie never had the ability to speak at all.

Through watching Charlie Ben from birth to death, I learned that in "Sepulchre of Songs," I got it right. Elaine, given the choice, would go to where she could be free of her body. While there really are people like the therapist, who had come to love her through serving her and would devote himself to her even when, one way or another, she had left him behind.